AF125230

Walter Bagehot

Parliamentary Reform

Anatiposi

Walter Bagehot

Parliamentary Reform

Reprint of the original, first published in 1859.

1st Edition 2023 | ISBN: 978-3-38231-280-0

Anatiposi Verlag is an imprint of Outlook Verlagsgesellschaft mbH.

Verlag (Publisher): Outlook Verlag GmbH, Zeilweg 44, 60439 Frankfurt, Deutschland
Vertretungsberechtigt (Authorized to represent): E. Roepke, Zeilweg 44, 60439 Frankfurt, Deutschland
Druck (Print): Books on Demand GmbH, In de Tarpen 42, 22848 Norderstedt, Deutschland

PARLIAMENTARY REFORM.

AN ESSAY.

BY

WALTER BAGEHOT.

REPRINTED, WITH CONSIDERABLE ADDITIONS, FROM THE NATIONAL REVIEW.

LONDON:

CHAPMAN AND HALL, 193 PICCADILLY.

[*Price Two Shillings.*]

PARLIAMENTARY REFORM.*

WE shall not be expected to discuss in a party spirit the subject of Parliamentary Reform. It has never been objected to the NATIONAL REVIEW that it is a party organ; and even periodicals which have long been such, scarcely now discuss that subject in a party spirit. Both Whigs and Conservatives are pledged to do something, and neither as a party have agreed what they would do. We would attempt to give an impartial criticism of the electoral system which now exists, and some indication of the mode in which we think that its defects should be amended. It is possible, we fear, that our article may be long, and that our criticism on existing arrangements may appear tedious. But a preliminary understanding is requisite; unless we are agreed as to what is to be desired, we cannot hope to agree as to what is to be done: a clear knowledge of the disease must precede the remedy. In business, no ingenuity of detail can compensate for indistinctness of design.

There is much that may be said against the Reform Act of 1832; but, on the whole, it has been successful. It is a commonplace to speak of the legislative improvements of the last twenty-five years, and it would be tedious to enumerate them. Free trade, a new colonial policy, the improved poor-law, the encumbered-estate act in Ireland, the tithe commutation, municipal reform, the tentative but most judicious support of education, are only some of the results of the reform of the House of Commons. Scarcely less important is the improvement which the Reform Bill has introduced into the general tone of our administration; our executive has become purer, more considerate, and more humane, and it would be difficult to show that in its ordinary and beneficial action it is much weaker. Nor is this all. So much of agreement in opinion as we see around us is perhaps unexampled in a political age; and it is the more singular, because the English nation is now considerably less homogeneous

---

* On the Electoral Statistics of the Counties and Boroughs in England and Wales during the Twenty-five Years from the Reform Act of 1832 to the Present Time. By William Newmarch, one of the Honorary Secretaries of the Statistical Society. Read before the Statistical Society, 16th June 1857, and printed in the Journal of that Society, Vol. XX. Parts II. and III.—We cannot speak too highly of these most admirable statistics. No pains have been spared to make them complete, and extreme judgment has been shown in the selection. When it is not otherwise stated, all our electoral statistics are from this source.

in its social structure than it was once. The prodigious growth of manufactures and trade has created a new world in the north of England, which contrasts with the south in social circumstances and social habits: at no former time was there such a difference as there now is between Lancashire and Devonshire. It is impossible not to ascribe this agreement to the habit of national discussion which the Reform Act has fostered. The scattered argument, the imperfect but perpetual influence of the press and society, have made us, perhaps even to an excessive degree, unanimous. Possibly we are all too much disposed to catch the voice which is in the air. Still, a little too much concord is better than a little too much discord. It is a striking result, that our present constitution has educed from such dissimilar elements so much of harmony.

Beneficial, however, as are these incidental results of the Reform Bill, they are not the most important parts of its success. This measure has, to a considerable extent, been successful in its *design*. The object which its framers had in view was, to transfer the predominant influence in the state from certain special classes to the general aggregate of fairly instructed men. It is not perhaps very easy to prove upon paper that this has been, at least in a very great degree, effected. The most difficult thing to establish by argument is an evident fact of observation. There are no statistics of opinion to which we can refer, there is no numerical comparison which will establish the accordance of parliamentary with social opinion. We must trust to our eyes and ears, to the vague but conclusive evidence of events. If, indeed, public opinion had always been as unanimous as it now is, we should have some difficulty in ascertaining the fact. When every body thinks the same, there is no saying which is the stronger party. But during the last twenty-six years there have been many periods at which public opinion was much divided and strongly excited. The great legislative changes which have been mentioned were not effected without long and animated party dissension. The policy of a great country like this has continually required the determination of critical questions, both at home and abroad; its ramified affairs have been a never-failing source of controverted topics. What would have been the sign if the expressed opinion of Parliament had been contrary to the distinct opinion of the country? In the present state of the country we should not have been long in learning it. We should have had political meetings, not of one class but all classes, clouds of petitions from every quarter, endless articles in newspapers; the cry would only have died away when the obnoxious decision was reversed, and the judgment of Parliament submitted itself to the will of the nation. The inclination of the House of Commons is evidently not to oppose the country. On the contrary, we all know the power, the undue power, possessed by that part of the press whose course is supposed to indicate what is likely to be the common opinion. So far from our legislators dissenting too often from the expressed judgment of the country, they are but too much swayed by indications of what it probably will be.—The history of our great legislative changes, of itself shows that the opinion of Parliament is, in the main, coincident with that of the nation. Parliament and the country were converted at the same time. Even the history of the corn-law agitation, which is often referred to as indicating the contrary, proves this conspicuously. It succeeded almost at the moment that impartial people, who had no interests on either side, were convinced that it ought to succeed. Mr. Cobden liked to relate, that when he first began to dream of agitating the question, a most experienced nobleman observed to him, "Repeal the Corn-laws! you will repeal the monarchy as soon." The noble lord was right in estimating the tenacity and intensity of the protectionist creed; but he did not know, and Mr. Cobden did, the power of plain argument on the common mass of plain men, and the certainty that *their* opinion, if really changed, would suffice to change the course of our legislation, even in opposition to strong aristocratic influence and very rooted prejudice. It has been said that Sir Robert Peel owed his success in life to "being converted at the conversion of the average man;" the same influences acted on his mind that acted on the minds of most other people throughout the nation, and in much the same measure. He was, therefore, converted to new views at the same time that most other people were converted to them. The same may be said of the present Parliament. Nobody would call the reformed House of Commons original; it is never in advance of the higher order of cultivated thought: but every one would agree that it is preëminently considerate, well-judging, and convincible; and when people say this, they mean that its opinions commonly coincide with their own.

In no respect is the reality of the accordance in opinion between Parliament and the nation so convincingly shown as in the sympathy of Parliament with the eccentricities of public opinion. We are constantly acknowledging that "the English mind" is exclusively occupied with single questions; sometimes with one, and sometimes with another, but at each time with one only. If Parliament did not share the same influences as the general body of fairly educated men, there would every now and then be a remarkable contrast between the subjects which interested Parliament and that which occupied the nation. The intensity of our peculiar sympathies makes this more likely.

Satirists say that the English nation is liable to intellectual *seizures;* and so exclusive and so restless is our intellectual absorption, so sudden its coming, so quick sometimes is its cessation, that there is some significance in the phrase. We are struck with particular ideas, and for the time think of nothing else. It will be found that Parliament, if it be sitting, thinks of the same. No instance of this can be more remarkable than the parliamentary proceedings on Mr. Roebuck's motion for an inquiry into the conduct of the Crimean campaign. There was great excitement in the nation at the moment; it has enabled the present generation to understand what historians did not before understand—the fate of poor Admiral Byng. The English nation cannot bear failure in war. If there had been any one to hang at the time Mr. Roebuck made his motion, and he could have been hung directly, certainly he would have been hung. On the other hand, the authority of statesmanlike opinion in Parliament, the weight of political connection, the legitimate disinclination to break up a government during a dangerous crisis, and—what is more remarkable—the great preponderance of sound argument, were united to influence Parliament not to grant even an inquiry. The result showed that the opinion of our leading statesmen was right, and that the arguments they produced were incontrovertible. Few investigations that have been commenced with so much outcry have ever had so trivial an effect. Yet, in opposition to all these influences, usually so omnipotent,—in opposition to the combined force of personal feeling and abstract argument,—the House of Commons so far accurately represented the sentiment of the country as to grant, and even to insist on granting, the inquiry. This parliamentary episode appears to be an *instantia lucifera* on the subject; it shows that, even when we could wish it otherwise, the House of Commons will echo the voice of the nation.

After all, there can be no more conclusive evidence of the substantial agreement between Parliament and the nation than the slight interest which is taken by the public in all questions of organic reform. Every one knows how the Reform Act of 1832 was carried; no one doubted that the public mind was excited then; no fair person could doubt what the decision of the nation then was. The "insurrection of the middle classes," as it has been called, ensured the success of the "Bill." It was alleged by its most reasonable opponents "that the measure could not be final; that those on whom it was proposed to confer the franchise would, even after the passing of the measure, be but small in comparison with those from whom it would be still withheld; that in a few years a similar agitation would recur, and a similar necessity of yielding to agitation;

that the storm of 1832 would be a feeble prelude to that of 1842," &c. These prophecies were not without a species of probability, but they have not been realised. No excited multitude clamours for enfranchisement; the reality is the reverse of the anticipation.

Two defects, however, may be discerned in the general accordance of parliamentary with national opinion. The Parliament certainly has an undue bias towards the sentiments and views of the landed interest. It is not easy to trace this in immediate results. We have said that we scarcely think that it is proved by the history of the free-trade agitation; that agitation was successful nearly, if not quite, as soon as it should have been. We may, indeed, speculate on the results which might have occurred if the Irish famine had not happened, and if Sir R. Peel had not formed a statesmanlike judgment upon its consequences; we may believe that there would in that case have been an opposition between an educated nation converted by reasoning to the principles of free trade, and a majority in Parliament wedded by prejudice and interest to protection. Still, as this is but conjecture, we cannot cite it as conclusive evidence. Nor is the partiality to real property in matters of taxation which is occasionally dwelt on very easy to prove in figures. The account is at best a complicated one. The exemption of land from probate duty is partly compensated by the succession duty, by the land-tax, by the more severe pressure of the income-tax, and still more by the necessary incidence of much local taxation on this kind of property. Still, a fair observer, closely comparing the opinion of the House of Commons with that of the public out of doors, will certainly observe some signs of a partiality towards the landed interest among our legislators. We cannot ascribe this to any obvious preponderance in number of the county over the borough seats. Taking population as a test, it is otherwise. There are in England and Wales 159 county members, more than double that number (viz. 335) of borough members; the population of the represented boroughs is 7,500,000, that of the counties 10,500,000, consequently the represented boroughs have not as many inhabitants as the counties, though they elect twice the number of members. This test is, of course, a most imperfect one; but it may serve to show that in mere arithmetic the counties are not extravagantly favoured. The real cause is the peculiar structure of our county society. A county member is almost of necessity one of the county gentry; he must not only possess land, but it must be land in that place: no one else is " entitled to stand." On the other hand, boroughs return a very miscellaneous class of members. Many important landowners sit for them. So great is the variety, that no class is excluded from them altogether. This con-

trast must affect the distribution of parliamentary power. The
county members form a peculiar class in the House of Commons, and exercise a steady influence there out of proportion to
their mere numbers. Besides, so much more of social influence
belongs to the territorial aristocracy than to any other class,
that its weight is indefinitely increased. Not a few men enter
Parliament mainly to augment their social importance, and over
these the unquestioned possessors of social rank necessarily have
great power. A third circumstance contributes its effect. The
ministers of the crown are generally large landowners. By im-
perious social usage, they must be men of large property; and
all opulence gravitates towards the land. Political opulence
does so particularly. Until recently there was much difficulty
in finding other investments not requiring sedulous personal attention, and not liable to be affected by political vicissitudes. It
is of essential importance that ministers of state should be persons *at ease* in their worldly circumstances, and it is quite out of
the question that they should have any share in the administration of commercial enterprises; they have enough to do without
that. Their wealth too should not be in a form that could expose
them even to the suspicion of stock-jobbing, or of making an improper use of political information. We have now many kinds
of property debentures, canal shares, railway shares, &c., which
have these advantages in nearly an equal degree with land
itself; but the growth of these is recent. It may hereafter have
important consequences, but it has not as yet had time to achieve
them. Accordingly the series of cabinet ministers presents a
nearly unbroken rank of persons who either are themselves large
landowners, or are connected closely by birth or intermarriage
with large landowners. This combination of circumstances gives
to real property an influence in our political system greater than
in strict theory we should wish it to have. It is true that the
owners of much land are men of much leisure, and the possession of such property has a sedative influence, which in modera-
tion may not be undesirable; but the effective representation of
national opinion requires the selection of members of parliament
from men of various occupations, various tendencies, and various
sympathies. Public opinion in a composite nation is formed by
the action and reaction of many kinds of minds; and abstract-
edly it seems a defect that the solid mass of county members, on
whatever side of the house they sit, should present features so
marked and uniform.

The second defect in the accordance of parliamentary with
national opinion is but another phase of the same fact. Too
little weight is at present given to the growing parts of the country, too much to the stationary. It appears that the county

constituencies in England and Wales have only increased, in the twenty years between 1837 and 1857, from 473,000 to 505,000, that is, at about six per cent; the borough constituencies, in the same period, have increased from 321,000 to 439,000, or at the rate of seventeen per cent. And it further appears, as we should expect, that the principal increase, both in the case of counties and boroughs, is not in the purely agricultural districts, but in the great scenes of manufacturing industry and in the metropolis. The growth of constituencies, according to the present franchise, is a much better test of relative importance than the mere growth of population; it indicates the increase of property, and therefore of presumable intelligence. These figures plainly indicate, if not an existing defect, yet a source of future defect in our representative system. If there was a just proportion between the two halves of England in 1832, there is not that just proportion now. In the long-run, public opinion will be much more influenced by the growing portion of the country than by the stationary. It is an indistinct perception of this fact that stimulates whatever agitation for reform at present exists. The manufacturers of Leeds and Manchester do not give levees and entertainments to Mr. Bright from any attraction to abstract democracy; the rate-paying franchise which Mr. Bright desires would place these classes under the irresistible control of their work-people. What our great traders really desire is, their own due weight in the community. They feel that the country squire and the proprietor of a petty borough have an influence in the nation above that which they ought to have, and greater than their own. A system arranged a quarter of a century ago presses with irritating constraint on those who have improved with half-magical rapidity during that quarter of a century,—is unduly favourable to those who have improved much less or not at all.

Subject, however, to these two exceptions, the House of Commons of the present day coincides nearly—or sufficiently nearly—in habitual judgment with the fairly intelligent and reasonably educated part of the community. Almost all persons, except the avowed holders of the democratic theory, would think that this is enough. Most people wish to see embodied in Parliament the *true judgment* of the nation; they wish to see an elected legislature fairly representing—that is, coinciding in opinion with—the thinking part of the community. What more, they would inquire, is wanted? We answer, that though this is by much the most important requisite of a good popular legislature, it is not absolutely the only one.

At present, the most important function of the representative part of our legislature—the House of Commons—is the *ruling* function. By a very well-known progress of events, the popular part of our constitution has grown out of very small beginnings to a practical sovereignty over all the other parts. To possess the confidence of the House of Commons is all that a minister desires; the power of the crown is reduced to a kind of social influence; that of the House of Lords is contracted to a suspensive veto. For the exercise of this ruling function, the substantial conformity of the judgment and opinion of the House of Commons with that of the fairly cultivated and fairly influential part of the people at large is the most important of possible conditions,—is, in fact, the one condition on which the satisfactory performance of that function appears to depend. No legislature destitute of this qualification, whatever its other merits may be, can create that feeling of diffused satisfaction which is the peculiar happiness of constitutional countries, or can ensure that distinct comprehension of a popular policy which is the greatest source of their strength. Nothing can satisfy which is not comprehended: no policy can be popular which is not understood. This is a truth of every-day observation. We are, nowadays, so familiar with the beneficial results of the ruling action of Parliament, that we are engrossed by it; we fancy that it is the sole duty of a representative assembly: yet so far is this from being the case, that in England it was not even the original one.

The earliest function of a House of Commons was undeniably what we may call an *expressive* function. In its origin it was (matters of taxation excepted) a petitioning body; all the early statutes, as is well known, are in this form: the Petition of Right is an instance of its adoption in times comparatively recent. The function of the popular part of the legislature was then to represent to the king the *wants* of his faithful commons. They were called to express the feelings of those who sent them and their own. Of course, in its original form, this function is obsolete; and if something analogous to it were not a needful element in the duties of every representative assembly, it would be childish to refer to it. But in every free country it is of the utmost importance,—and, in the long-run, a pressing necessity,—that all opinions extensively entertained, all sentiments widely diffused, should be *stated* publicly before the nation. We may place the real decision of questions, the actual adoption of policies, in the ordinary and fair intelligence of the community, or in the legislature which represents it. But we must also take care to bring before that fair intelligence and that legislature the sentiments, the interests, the opinions, the prejudices, the wants, of all classes of the nation; we must be sure that no decision is come to in ignorance of real facts and intimate wants. The diffused multitude of moderate men, whose opinions, taken in the aggregate, form public opinion, are just as likely to be tyrannical towards what they do not realise, inapprehensive of what is not argued out, thoughtless of what is not brought before them, as any other class can be. They will judge well of what they are made to understand; they will not be harsh to feelings that are brought home to their imagination; but the materials of a judgment must be given them, the necessary elements of imagination must be provided, otherwise the result is certain. A free government is the most stubbornly stupid of all governments to whatever is *unheard* by its deciding classes. On this account it is of the utmost importance that there should be in the House of Commons some persons able to speak, and authorised to speak, the wants, sentiments, and opinions of every section of the community—delegates, one might almost say, of that section. It is only by argument in the legislature that the legislature can be impressed; it is by argument in the legislature that the attention of the nation is most easily attracted and most effectually retained.

If, with the light of this principle, we examine our present system of representation, it seems unquestionable that it is defective. We do not provide any mode of expression for the sentiments of what are vaguely but intelligibly called the working classes. We ignore them. The Reform Act of 1832 assumed that it was expedient to give a representation to the wants and feelings of those who live in ten-pound houses, but that it was not expedient to give any such expression to the wants and feelings of those who live in houses rated below that sum. If we were called to consider that part of this subject, we should find much to excuse the framers of that act in the state of opinion which then prevailed and the general circumstances of the time. It was necessary to propose a simple measure; and this numerical demarcation has a trenchant simplicity. But if we now considerately review our electoral organisation, we must concede that, however perfectly it may provide an appropriate regulator for our national affairs, it omits to provide a befitting organ of *expression* for the desires and convictions of these particular classes.

The peculiar characteristics of a portion of the working classes render this omission of special importance. The agricultural labourers may have no sentiments on public affairs; but the artisan classes have. Not only are their circumstances peculiar, and their interests sometimes different from those of the higher orders of the community,—both which circumstances are likely to make them adopt special opinions, and are therefore grounds for a special representation,—but the habit of mind which their pursuits and position engender is of itself not unlikely to cause some eccentricity of judgment. Observers tell us that those who live by manual ingenuity are more likely to be

remarkable for originality than for modesty. In the present
age,—and to some extent, we must expect, in every age,—such
persons must be self-taught; and self-taught men are commonly
characterised by a one-sided energy and something of a self-suf-
ficient disposition. The *sensation* of perfection in a mechanical
employment is of itself not without an influence tending towards
conceit; and however instructed in definite learning energetic
men in these classes may become, they are not subjected to the
insensible influences of cultivated life, they do not live in the
temperate zone of society, which soon chills the fervid ideas
of unseasonable originality. Being cooped up within the nar-
row circle of ideas that their own energy has provided, they
are particularly liable to singular opinions. This is especially
the case on politics. They are attracted to that subject in a
free country of necessity; their active intellects are in search
of topics for reflection; and this subject abounds in the very
atmosphere of our natural life, is diffused in newspapers, ob-
truded at elections, to be heard at every corner of the street.
Energetic minds in this class are therefore particularly likely
to entertain eccentric opinions on political topics; and it is
peculiarly necessary that such opinions should, by some adequate machinery, be stated and made public. If such singular views be brought into daily collision with ascertained facts
and the ordinary belief of cultivated men, their worth can be
tested, the weakness of their fallacious part exposed, any new
grain of truth they may contain appreciated. On some subjects
(possibly, for example, on simple questions of foreign policy) the
views of self-taught men may be very valuable, for their moral
instincts sometimes have a freshness rarely to be found. At
any rate, whatever may be the abstract value of the special sentiments and convictions of the operative classes, their very speciality is a strong indication that our constitution is defective in
providing no distinct outlet for their expression.

A theorist might likewise be inclined to argue that the
Reform Act of 1832 was defective in not providing an appropriate organ for the expression of opinion of the higher orders of
society. It selects a ten-pound householder for special favour.
In large towns, nay to a certain extent in any town, the more
cultivated and refined classes, who live in better houses than
these, are practically disfranchised; the number of their inferiors
renders valueless the suffrage conferred on them. We remember
some years ago hearing a conversation between a foreigner and
a most accomplished Englishman who lived in Russell Square.
The foreigner was expatiating on the happiness of English people
in being governed by a legislature in which they were represented. The Russell-Square scholar replied, " *I* am represented

by Mr. Wakley and Tom Duncombe." He felt the scorn natural to a cultivated man in a metropolitan constituency at the supposition that such representatives as these really expressed *his* views and sentiments. We know how constantly in America, which is something like a nation of metropolitan constituencies, the taste and temper of the electors excludes the more accomplished and leisured classes from the legislature, and how vulgar a stamp the taste and temper of those elected impresses on the proceedings of its legislature and the conduct of its administration. Men of refinement shrink from the House of Representatives as from a parish vestry. In England, though we feel this in some measure, we feel it much less. Other parts of our electoral system now afford a refuge to that refined cultivation which is hateful to and hates the grosser opinion of the small shopkeepers in cities. Our higher classes still desire to rule the nation; and so long as this is the case, the inherent tendencies of human nature secure them the advantage. Manner and bearing have an influence on the poor; the nameless charm of refinement tells; personal confidence is almost every where more easily accorded to one of the higher classes than to one of the lower classes. From this circumstance, there is an inherent tendency in any electoral system which does not vulgarise the government to protect the rich and to represent the rich. Though by the letter of the law, a man who lives in a house assessed at 10*l.* has an equal influence on the constitution of the legislature with a man whose house is assessed at 100*l.*, yet, in truth, the richer man has the security that the members of Parliament, and especially the foremost members of Parliament, are much more likely to be taken from his class than from a poorer class.

We may therefore conclude that there is not any ground for altering the electoral system established by the Reform Act of 1832 on account of its not providing for the due representation of the more cultivated classes. Indirectly it does so. But we must narrowly watch any changes in that system which are proposed to us, with the view of seeing whether their operation might not have a tendency to impair the subtle working of this indirect machinery. We must bear in mind that the practical disfranchisement of the best classes is the ascertained result of giving an equal weight to high and low in constituencies like the metropolitan.

These considerations do not affect our previous conclusion as to the lower orders. We ascertained that, however perfectly the House of Commons under the present system of election may coincide in judgment with the fairly educated classes of the country, and however competent it may on that account be to perform the ruling function of a popular legislature, it was nevertheless defective in its provision for the performance of the *expressive* functions of such a legislature; because it provided no organ for informing Parliament and the country of the sentiments and opinions of the working, and especially of the artisan classes.

Another deficiency in the system of representation now existing is of a different nature. It is not only desirable that a popular legislature should be fitted to the discharge of its duties, but also that it should be elected by a process which occasions no unnecessary moral evils. A theorist would be inclined to advance a step further. He would require that a popular assembly should be elected in the mode which would diffuse the instruction given by the habitual possession of the franchise among the greatest number of competent persons, and which would deny it to the greatest number of unfit persons. But every reasonable theorist would hasten to add, that the end must never be sacrificed to the means. The mode of election which is selected must be one which will bring together an assembly of members fitted to discharge the functions of Parliament. *Among* those modes of election, this theoretical principle prescribes the rule of choice; but we must not, under its guidance, attempt to travel beyond the circle of those modes. A practical statesman will be very cautious how he destroys a machinery which attains its essential object for the sake of an incidental benefit which might be expected from a different machinery. If we have a good legislature, he will say, let us not endanger its goodness for the sake of a possible diffusion of popular education. All sensible men would require that the advocates of such a measure should show beyond all reasonable doubt that the extension of the suffrage, which they recommend on this secondary ground, should not impair the attainment of the primary end for which *all* suffrage was devised. At the present moment, there certainly are many persons of substantial property and good education who do not possess the franchise, and to whom it would be desirable to give it, if they could be distinguished from others who are not so competent. A man of the highest education, who does not reside in a borough, may have large property in the funds, in railway shares, or any similar investment; but he will have no vote unless his house is rated above 50*l.* But, as we have said, we must not, from a theoretical desire to include such persons in our list of electors, run a risk of admitting also any large number of persons who would be unfit to vote, and thereby impairing the practical utility of Parliament. No such hesitation should, however, hold us back when peculiar moral evils can be proved to arise from a particular mode of election. If that be so, we ought on the instant to make the

most anxious search for some other mode of election not liable
to the same objection: we ought to run some risk; if another
mode of election can be suggested, apparently equal in efficiency,
which would not produce the same evils, we should adopt it at
once in place of the other. We must act on the spirit of faith
that what is morally wrong cannot be politically right.

This objection applies in the strongest manner to one portion
of our electoral system, namely, the smaller borough constituencies. We there intrust the franchise to a class of persons
few enough to be bought, and not respectable enough to refuse
to be bought. The disgraceful exposures of some of these
boroughs before election committees make it probable that the
same abuses exist in others: doubtless, too, we do not know the
worst. The worst constituencies are slow to petition, because
the local agents of both parties are aware of what would come to
light, and fear the consequent penalties. Enough, however, is
in evidence for us to act upon. Some of these small boroughs
are dependent on some great nobleman or man of fortune; and
this state is perhaps preferable to their preserving a vicious inde-
pendence: but even this state is liable to very many objections.
It is most advantageous that the nominal electors should be the
real electors. Legal fictions have a place in courts of law; it is
sometimes better or more possible to strain venerable maxims
beyond their natural meaning than to limit them by special
enactment: but legal fictions are very dangerous in the midst of
popular institutions and a genuine moral excitement. We speak
day by day of "shams;" and the name will be for ever applied
to modes of election which pretend to intrust the exclusive choice
to those who are known by every body never to choose. The
Reform Act of 1832 was distinctly founded on the principle that
all modes of election should be *real*.

We arrive, therefore, at the result that the system of 1832
is defective, because it established, or rather permitted to continue, moral evils which it is our duty to remove, if by possibility they can be removed. However, in that removal we must
be careful to watch exactly what we are doing. It has been
shown that the letter of the Reform Act makes no provision for
the special representation of wealth and cultivation; the representation which they have is attained by *indirect* means. The
purchasable boroughs are undoubtedly favourable to wealth;
the hereditary boroughs to men of hereditary cultivation; and
we should be careful not to impair unnecessarily the influence of
these elements by any alteration we may resolve upon.

We can now decide on the result which we should try to
attain in a new Reform Bill. If we could obtain a House of
Commons that should be well elected, that should contain true

and adequate exponents of all class interests, that should coincide in opinion with the fair intelligence of the country, we shall have all which we ought to desire. We have satisfied ourselves that we do not possess all these advantages now; we have seen that a part of our system of election is grossly defective; that our House of Commons contains no adequate exponents of the views of the working classes; that though its judgment has, as yet, fairly coincided with public opinion, yet that its constitution gives a dangerous preponderance to the landed interest, and is likely to fail us hereafter unless an additional influence be given to the more growing and energetic classes of society.

We should think it more agreeable (and perhaps it would be so to most of our readers) if we were able at once to proceed to discuss the practical plan by which these objects might be effected; but in deference to a party which has some zealous adherents, and to principles which, in an indistinct shape, are widely diffused, we must devote a few remarks to the consideration of the ultra-democratic theory; and as we have to do so, it will be convenient to discuss in connection with it one or two of the schemes which the opponents of that theory have proposed for testing political intelligence.

As is well known, the democratic theory requires that parliamentary representation should be proportioned to mere numbers. This is not, indeed, the proposition which is at this moment put forward. The most important section of democratic reformers now advocate a rate-paying or household franchise; but this is either avowedly as a step to something farther, or because from considerations of convenience it is considered better to give the franchise only to those whose residences can be identified. But it is easy to show that the rate-paying franchise is almost equally liable with the manhood suffrage to a most important objection. That objection, of course, is, that the adoption of the scheme would give entire superiority to the lower part of the community. Nothing is easier than to show that a rate-paying franchise would have that effect. In England and Wales

The number of houses assessed at 10*l.* and above is computed to be	. . . .	990,000
„	„	at 6*l.* and under 10*l.*	572,000
„	„	under 6*l.*	1,713,000
			3,275,000

More than half the persons who would be admitted by the rate-paying franchise are, therefore, of a very low order, living in houses under 6*l.* rent, and two-thirds are below 10*l.*, the lowest qualification admitted by the present law. It therefore seems quite certain that the effect of the proposed innovation must be very favourable to ignorance and poverty, and very unfavourable to cultivation and intelligence.

There used to be much argument in favour of the democratic theory, on the ground of its supposed conformity with the abstract rights of man. This has passed away; but we cannot say that the reasons by which it has been replaced are more distinct: we think that they are less distinct. We can understand that an enthusiast should maintain, on fancied grounds of immutable morality, or from an imaginary conformity with a supernatural decree, that the ignorant should govern the instructed; but we do not comprehend how any one can maintain the proposition on grounds of expediency. We might believe it was right to submit to the results of such a polity; but those results, it would seem, must be beyond controversy pernicious. The arguments from expediency, which are supposed to establish the proposition, are never set forth very clearly; and we do not think them worth confuting. We are, indeed, disposed to believe, in spite of much direct assertion to the contrary, that the democratic theory still rests not so much on reason as on a kind of sentiment—on an obscure conception of abstract rights. The animation of its advocates is an indication of it. They think they are contending for the "rights" of the people; and they endeavour to induce the people to believe so too. We hold this opinion the more strongly, because we believe that there *is* such a thing, after all, as abstract right in political organisations. We find it impossible to believe that all the struggles of men for liberty,—all the enthusiasm it has called forth, all the passionate emotions it has caused in the very highest minds, all the glow of thought and rustle of obscure feeling which the very name excites in the whole mass of men,— have their origin in calculations of advantage and a belief that such and such arrangements would be beneficial. The masses of men are very difficult to excite on bare grounds of self-interest; most easy, if a bold orator tells them confidently they are *wronged.* The foundation of government upon simple utility is but the fiction of philosophers; it has never been acceptable to the natural feelings of mankind. There is far greater truth in the formula of the French writers, that " *le droit dérive de la capacité.*" Some sort of feeling akin to this lurks, we believe, in the minds of our reformers; they think they can show that some classes now unenfranchised are as capable of properly exercising the franchise as some who have possessed it formerly, or some who have it now. The five-pound householder of to-day is, they tell us, in education and standing but what the ten-pound householder was in 1832. The opponents of the theory are pressed with the argument, that every fit person should have the franchise, and that many who are excluded are as fit as some who exercise it, and from whom no one proposes to take it away.

The answer to the argument is plain. Fitness to govern,—for that is the real meaning of exercising the franchise which elects a *ruling* assembly,—is not an absolute quality of any individual. That fitness is relative and comparative; it must depend on the community to be governed, and on the merits of other persons who may be capable of governing that community. A savage chief may be capable of governing a savage tribe; he may have the right of governing it, for he may be the sole person capable of so doing; but he would have no right to govern England. We must look likewise to the competitors for the sovereignty. Whatever may be your capacity for rule, you have no right to obtain the opportunity of exercising it by dethroning a person who is *more* capable. You are wronging the community if you do : for you are depriving it of a better government than that which you can give to it. You are wronging also the ruler you supersede; for you are depriving him of the appropriate exercise of his faculties. Two wrongs are thus committed from a fancied idea that abstract capacity gives a right to rule irrespective of comparative relations. The true principle is, that every person has a right to *so much political power as he can exercise without impeding any other person who would more fitly exercise such power.* If we apply this to the lower orders of society, we see the reason why, notwithstanding their numbers, they must always be subject— always at least be comparatively uninfluential. Whatever their capacity may be, it must be less than that of the higher classes, whose occupations are more instructive and whose education is more prolonged. Any such measure for enfranchising the lower orders as would overpower, and consequently disfranchise, the higher, should be resisted on the ground of " abstract right;" you are proposing to take power from those who have the superior capacity, and to vest it in those who have but an inferior capacity, or, in many cases, no capacity at all. If we probe the subject to the bottom, we shall find that justice is on the side of a graduated rule, in which all persons should have an influence proportioned to their political capacity; and it is at this graduation that the true maxims of representative government really aim. They wish that the fairly intelligent persons, who create public opinion, as we call it, in society, should rule in the state, which is the authorised means of carrying that opinion into action. This is the body which has the greater right to rule; this is the *felt intelligence* of the nation, " *la légitime aristocratie, celle qu'acceptent librement les masses, sur qui doit exercer son pouvoir.*"*

It is impossible to deny that this authority, in matters of

---

* M. Guizot, Essai sur les Origines du Gouvernement réprésentatif.

political opinion, belongs by right, and is felt to belong in fact, to the higher orders of society rather than to the lower. The advantages of leisure, of education, of more instructive pursuits, of more instructive society, must and do produce an effect. A writer of very democratic leanings has observed, that "there is an unconquerable, and, to a certain extent, beneficial proneness in man to rely on the judgment and authority of those who are elevated above himself in rank and riches, from the irresistible associations of the human mind; a feeling of respect and deference is entertained for a superior in station which enhances and exalts all his good qualities, gives more grace to his thoughts, more wisdom to his opinions, more weight to his judgment, more excellence to his virtues. . . . . Hence the elevated men of society will always maintain an ascendency which, without any direct exertion of influence, will affect the result of popular elections; and when to this are added the capabilities which they possess, or ought to possess, from their superior intelligence, of impressing their own opinions on other classes, it will be evident that if any sort of control were justifiable, it would be superfluous for any good purpose."* There are individual exceptions; but in questions of this magnitude we must speak broadly: and we may say that political intelligence will in general exist rather in the educated classes than in the less educated, rather in the rich than the poor; and not only that it will exist, but that it will, in the absence of misleading feelings, be *felt* by both parties to exist.

We have quoted the above passage for more reasons than one. It not only gives an appropriate description of the popular association of superiority in judgment with superiority in station, but it draws from the fact of that association an inference which would be very important if it were correct. It says, in substance, that as the higher orders are felt by the lower to be more capable of governing, they will be chosen by the lower, if the latter are left free to choose; that, therefore, no matter how democratic the government—in fact, the more democratic the government, the surer are the upper orders to lead. But experience shows that this is an error. If the acquisition of power is left to the unconscious working of the natural influences of society, the rich and the cultivated will certainly acquire it; they obtain it insensibly, gradually, and without the poorer orders knowing that they are obtaining it. But the result is different when, by the operation of a purely democratic constitution, the selection of rulers is submitted to the direct vote of the populace. The lower orders are then told that they are perfectly able to judge; demagogues assert it to them without ceasing: the con-

* Bailey on Representative Government; quoted in Sir G. Lewis's "Essay on the Influence of Authority in Matters of Opinion," p. 228.

stitution itself is appealed to as an incontrovertible witness to the fact; as it has placed the supreme power in the hands of the lower and more numerous classes, it would be contravening it to suppose that the real superiority was in the higher and fewer. Moreover, when men are expressly asked to acknowledge their superiors, they are by no means always inclined to do so. They do not object to yield a mute observance, but they refuse a definite act of homage. They will obey, but they will not *say* that they will obey. In consequence, history teaches that under a democratic government those who speak the feelings of the majority themselves have a greater chance of being chosen to rule, than any of the higher orders, who, under another form of government, would be admitted to be the better judges. The natural effect of such a government is to mislead the poor.

We have no room to notice the specific evils which would accrue from the adoption of an unmixedly democratic constitution. One, however, which has not been quite appreciated follows naturally from the remarks we have made. There is a risk of vulgarising the whole tone, method, and conduct of public business. We see how completely this has been done in America; a country far more fitted, at least in the northern states, for the democratic experiment than any old country can be. Nor must we imagine that this vulgarity of tone is a mere external expression, not affecting the substance of what is thought, or interfering with the policy of the nation. No defect really eats away so soon the political ability of a nation. A vulgar tone of discussion disgusts cultivated minds with the subject of politics; they will not apply themselves to master a topic which, besides its natural difficulties, is encumbered with disgusting phrases, low arguments, and the undisguised language of coarse selfishness. We all know how we should like to interfere in ward elections, borough politics, or any public matter over which a constant habit of half-educated discussion has diffused an atmosphere of deterring associations. A high morality, too, shrinks with the inevitable shyness of superiority from intruding itself into the presence of low debates. The inevitable consequence of vulgarising our Parliament would be the deterioration of public opinion, not only in its more refined elements, but in all the tangible benefits we derive from the application to politics of thoroughly cultivated minds.

Nor can we allude to the refutation of the purely democratic theory which the facts of English history supply us. It is frequently something like pedantry when reference is made to the origin of the House of Commons as a source of *data* for deciding on the proper constitution for it now. What might have been a proper constitution for it when an inconsiderable part of the government, may be a most improper one now that it is the ruling part. Still, one brief remark may be advanced as to the early history of our representative system, which will have an important reference to the topic. "Whilst," writes one of our soundest constitutional antiquaries, "boroughs were thus reluctant to return members, and burgesses disinclined to serve in that capacity, the sheriffs assumed a right of sending or omitting precepts at their pleasure. Where boroughs were unwilling or unable to send representatives, the sheriff, from favour or indulgence, withheld the precept, which in strictness he was bound to issue, and thus acquired a discretionary power of settling what places were to elect, and what places were not to elect, members of Parliament. In his return to the writ of summons, he sometimes reported that he had sent his precept to a borough, but had received no answer to it. Sometimes he asserted, without the slightest regard to truth, that there were no more cities or boroughs in his bailiwick than those mentioned in his return. At other times he qualified this assertion by adding that there were none fit to send members to Parliament, or that could be induced to send them. No notice seems ever to have been taken of these proceedings of the sheriffs; nor is there the slightest ground for suspecting that in the exercise of his discretionary power he was directed by any secret instructions from the king and council : ' I have never seen or heard,' says Brady, ' of any particular directions from the king and council or others to the sheriffs, for sending their precepts to this or that borough only and not to others.' *Provided there was a sufficient attendance of members for the public business, the government seem to have been indifferent to the number that came, or to the number of places from which they were sent."** The public business of that time was different from the public business which is now transacted by Parliament; but we may paraphrase the sentence into one that is applicable to us. Provided we have a House of Commons coinciding in opinion with the general mass of the public, and containing representatives competent to express the peculiar sentiments of all peculiar classes, we have provided for our "public business;" we need not trouble ourselves much further, we shall have attained all reasonable objects of desire, and established a polity with which we may be content.

The most obvious way of attempting this is, to represent, or attempt to represent, intelligence directly. The simplest plan of embodying public opinion in a legislature, is to give a special representation in that legislature, to the politically intelligent persons who create that opinion. To attain this end directly is, however, impossible. There is no test of intelligence which a revising barrister could examine, on which attorneys could argue before him. The absurdity of the idea is only rendered

* Allen on Parliamentary Reform, 1832.

more evident by the few proposals which are made in the hope of realising it. Mr. Holyoake proposes that the franchise should be given to those who could pass a political examination; an examination, that is, in some standard text-book,—Mill's *Principles of Political Economy,* or some work of equal reputation. But it does not need to be explained that this would enfranchise extremely few people in a country. Only a few persons give, or can give, a scientific attention to politics; and very many who cannot, are in every respect competent to give their votes as electors, and even to serve as representatives. It is probable that the adoption of such an examination suffrage, in addition to the kinds of suffrage which exist now, would not add one per cent to the present constituencies; and that if it were made a necessary qualification for the possession of a vote, we should thereby disfranchise ninety-nine hundredths of the country. A second proposal with the same object is, to give votes to all members of "learned societies." But this would be contemptibly futile. There is no security whatever that members of learned societies should be really learned. They are close corporations; and the only check on the admission of improper persons in future is the discretion of those who have been admitted already. At present most members of such societies undoubtedly have an interest in the objects for which they were formed; but create a political motive, and a skilful parliamentary agent will soon fill the lists with the names of persons not celebrated for scientific learning, but who know how to vote correctly upon occasion. The idea of a direct representation of intelligence wholly fails from the non-existence of a visible criterion of that intelligence. All that can be done in this direction must be effected by a gradual extension of the principle which has given members to our Universities. No one can obtain admission to these bodies without a prolonged course of study, or without passing a strict examination in several subjects. This is a kind of franchise not to be manufactured; it is only obtained as a collateral advantage, by persons who are in pursuit of quite different objects. Such bodies, however, are obviously few, and such kinds of franchise are necessarily limited. But they should be extended as far as possible; and as many such bodies as can be found will tend to supply us with an additional mode of giving a representation to cultivation and refinement,—an object which we noticed as one of the desirable ends apparently least provided for by the letter of our present system.*

* In relation to this subject, we must call special attention to the claims of the University of London and, of the Scotch Universities to representation in Parliament. The former University had a distinct pledge from the Government which founded it that it should be placed on an equality in every respect with

The criteria by which a franchise can be determined must have two characteristics. They must be evident and conspicuous —tests about which there can be no question. Our registration courts cannot decide metaphysical niceties ; our machinery must be tough, if it is to stand the wear and tear of eager contests. Secondly, as we have explained, such criteria must be difficult to manufacture for a political object. Our tests must not be counterfeited, and they must be conspicuous. These two requirements nearly confine us to a property qualification. Property is, indeed, a very imperfect test of intelligence; but it is some test. If it has been inherited, it guarantees education; if acquired, it guarantees ability. Either way it assures us of something. In all countries where any thing has prevailed short of manhood suffrage, the principal limitation has been founded on criteria derived from property. And it is very important to observe that there is a special appropriateness in the selection. Property has not only a certain connection with general intelligence, but it has a peculiar connection with *political* intelligence. It is a great guide to a good judgment to have much to lose by a bad judgment. Generally speaking, the welfare of a country will be most dear to those who are well off there. Some considerations, it is true, may limit this principle : great wealth has an emasculating tendency; the knowledge that they have much at stake may make men timid in action, and too anxious, for the successful discharge of high duties : still the broad conclusion is unaffected, that the possession of property is not only an indication of general mind, but has a peculiar tendency to generate *political mind*.

Similar considerations limit the kinds of property to be selected. Our property qualification must be conspicuous and uncreateable. Real property,—houses and land,—on which our present qualification is based, possess these elements in a preeminent degree. We think, however, that they are not the only kinds of property which now in a sufficient degree possess these requirements. They probably were so formerly ; but one of the most important alterations in our social condition is the change in the nature of much of our wealth. The growth of what lawyers call personal property has of late years been enormous. Rail-

Oxford and Cambridge. And such Universities would not only introduce additional representatives of intellectual culture into the House of Commons, but representatives also of *free* intellectual culture, as distinguished from the representatives of the ecclesiastical culture of the older Universities. Mr. Bright has reproached the members for Oxford and Cambridge Universities with their habitual antagonism to Reform. This is, we fear, a true accusation. At a time when educational questions are engrossing a larger and larger share of public attention, an adequate representation of *liberal* intellectual culture is most desirable in the House of Commons.

way shares, canal shares, public funds, bank shares, debentures without number, are only instances of what we mean. Great industrial undertakings are a feature in our age, and it is fitting that a share in them should give a franchise as much as an estate in land. Two conditions only would be necessary to be observed. First, the property must be substantial, as it is called; that is to say, it should be remunerative. Property which does not yield an income is not sufficiently tangible for the purposes of a qualification: men of business may say it is *about* to yield a dividend; but this is always open to infinite argument. It would be necessary to provide that the business property to be represented should have been for a moderate period—say three years —properly remunerative; no one should register for such property unless it had for that period paid a regular interest. Secondly, such property should have been in the possession of the person wishing to register on account of it for at least an equal previous period. This is necessary to prevent the creation of fictitious votes. Real property is, indeed, exposed to this danger; but the occupancy of houses and lands is a very visible fact, and acts of ownership over the soil are tolerably well known on the spot. It is therefore somewhat difficult to create fictitious tenancies or freeholds. In the case of share-property there is no equal check. The only precaution which can be taken is, to make the pecuniary risk of those who try to create such votes as large as possible. If it be required that the property be registered for a moderate period in the company's books as belonging to the person who claims to vote in respect of it, that person must have during that time the sole right to receive the dividends, and the shares will be liable for all his debts. If a real owner chooses to put a nominal one in this position, he does it at the risk of both principal and income.

We have, then, arrived at the end of another division of our subject. We have shown that the democratic theory is erroneous, and that the consequences of acting upon it would be pernicious. We have discussed the most plausible schemes which have been suggested for testing political intelligence, and we have found reason to think that a property qualification is the best of those modes. It has incidentally appeared that the property qualification which at present exists in England is defective, because it only takes cognisance of a single kind of property. We may now resume the thread of our discussion, which we laid aside to show the errors of the democratic theory. We proceed to indicate how the defects which have been proved to be parts of our existing system of representation can be remedied without impairing its characteristic excellence, without destroying a legislature which is in tolerable conformity with intelligent opinion.

The first defect which we noticed was, that the existing system takes no account of the views and feelings of the working classes, and affords no means for their expression. How, then, can this be supplied? It is evident that this end can only be approached in two ways; we may give to the working classes a *little* influence in all constituencies, or we may give to them a good deal of influence in a few constituencies. By the conditions of the problem they are to have some power in the country, but not all the power; and these are the only two modes in which that end can be effected.

The objection to the first plan is in the nature of a dilemma. Either your arrangements give to the working classes a sufficient power to enable them to decide the choice of the member, or they do not. If they do, they make these classes absolute in the state. If the degree of influence which you grant to them in *every* constituency is sufficient to enable them to choose the representative for that constituency, you have conferred on these inferior classes the unlimited control of the nation. On the other hand, if the degree of influence you give to the poorer classes is not sufficient to enable them to control the choice of any members, you have done nothing. There will be no persons in Parliament inclined by nature and empowered by authority to express their sentiments; their voice will be as much unheard in Parliament as it is now. If the poor are to have a diffused influence in all constituencies, it must be either a great one or a small one. A small one will amount only to the right of voting for a candidate who is *not* elected; a great one will, in reality, be the establishment of democracy.

We shall see the truth of this remark more distinctly if we look a little in detail at one or two of the plans which are proposed with this object. Perhaps the most remarkable of these is that which is at present in operation in Prussia. The suffrage is there very diffused; it amounts to something very like manhood suffrage. But the influence of the lower classes is limited in this way: The constituency is divided into classes according to the amount of direct taxation they respectively pay. The names of those voters who pay the highest amount of tax are put together till a third part of the whole amount of direct taxes paid by the electoral district has been reached. These form the first class. Again, as many names are taken as will make up another third of the same total taxation; and these form the second class. The third class is formed of all the rest, and each class has an equal vote. By this expedient a few very rich persons in class 1, and a moderate number of moderately rich persons in class 2, have each of them as much influence as the entire number of the poorer orders in class 3. In Prussia a system of double representation has also been adopted, and for that purpose the constituency is divided into sections. But we need not confuse ourselves with prolix detail; the principle is all which is to the purpose. The effect of the plan is evident; it is equivalent to giving to the working classes *one-third* of the influence in every constituency, and no more than one-third. But it is evident that this arrangement not only gives no security for the return of a satisfactory spokesman for the lower orders, but that it provides that no such spokesman shall be returned. The two superior classes are two-thirds of the constituency, and they will take effectual care that no member animated solely with the views of the other third shall ever be elected. So far as class feeling goes, the power given to the lower orders is only the power of voting in a perpetual minority. Undoubtedly, in case of a division between the two superior classes, the lower orders would hold the balance; they would have the power in all constituencies of deciding who should and who should not be the member. But this is not the kind of influence which we have shown it to be desirable that the lower orders should possess. Nothing can be more remote from their proper sphere than the position of arbitrator between the conflicting views of two classes above them. We wish that they should have a few members to express their feelings; we do not wish that they should decide on the critical controversies of their educated fellow-subjects,— that they should determine by a casting and final vote the policy of the nation.

Another plan suggested is, that the lower orders should have a single vote, and that persons possessed of property should have a second vote. But statistics show that the power which this would give to the lower orders would be enormous. For example, if it should be enacted that all persons living in houses rated at less than 10*l.* shall have one vote, and that those living in houses rated at more than 10*l.*, two votes, we should have

990,000 living in houses of 10*l.* and more than 10*l.* } with 1,980,000 votes,
2,280,000 living in houses under 10*l.* . . . with 2,280,000 votes;

giving a clear majority throughout the country to the lowest class of rate-payers; and that majority would of course be much augmented if we conferred (as the advocates of manhood suffrage propose) a vote on every adult male in the country, whether he paid rates or not. The inevitable effect of this plan would be to give an authoritative control to the poorer classes. We might, indeed, try to obviate this by giving a still greater number of votes, say three or four, to the richer class; but then we should reduce the poorer class to an impotent minority throughout the country. In the first case, they would have the power of returning nearly all the members of the legislature; in the second, they would not as a class, or with an irresistible influence, return any.

Another scheme, proposed with this object, at least in part, is the "representation of minorities," as it is commonly called. This is to be attained by the ingenious device of making the number of votes to be possessed by each constituent less than the number of members to be returned by the constituency. The consequence is inevitable: an ascertainable minority of the constituency, by voting for a single candidate only, can effectually secure his election. Thus, if the number of members is three and the number of votes two, any fraction of the constituency greater than two-fifths can be sure of returning a member, if they are in earnest enough on the matter to vote for him only. The proof of this is, that a minority of two-fifths will have exactly as many votes to give to one member as the remaining three-fifths have to give to each of three members. If the constituency be 5000, a minority of two-fifths of the electors, or 2000, would have 2000 votes to give to a single candidate; and the remaining 3000 would have only 6000 votes to divide between three candidates, which is only 2000 for each. A minority at all greater than 2000, therefore, would, if it managed properly, be certain to return a member. The objection to this plan is, that it would rather tend to give us a Parliament principally elected by the lower orders, with special members among them to express the sentiments of the wealthier classes, than a Parliament generally agreeing with the wealthier classes, and containing special representatives for the lower: the principal representation is almost by express legislation given to the more numerous classes; a less to the minority. It would not solve the problem of giving a certain power to the lower orders, and yet not giving them a predominant power. In the case which we have supposed of a constituency with three members and two votes, the minority also would be a larger one than the richer classes can permanently hope to constitute in the country. Two-fifths of a great town must necessarily include many of the poorer, less cultivated, and less competent. We must remember, also, that the disproportion in number between rich and poor, even between the decidedly poor and the rather wealthy, tends to augment. Society increases most rapidly at its lower end; the wide base extends faster than the narrower summit. At present persons living in "ten-pound houses," or upwards, are something like 21 per cent of the adult males in the nation, and about 30 per cent of the rate-paying population. But in process of time the inevitable increase of the humbler orders will reduce them to a far more scanty proportion.

The operation of the plan might become even more defective if it were combined, as is often proposed, with an increase of the number of members returned by the constituencies to which it is to be applied. If four members were given to a populous constituency, and each elector were to have three votes, it would require that a minority should be more than three-sevenths* of the constituency, to enable it to be certain of returning a candidate. The rich and educated cannot expect to remain so large a fraction of the nation as this; they are not so now.

The most plausible way of embodying the minority principle in action would be to give only one vote to each person, and only *two* members to the constituency. In this case, any minority greater than one-third of the constituency would be sure of returning a member; and as this fraction is smaller than those we have mentioned, it would evidently be more suitable to the inevitable fewness of the rich and intelligent. But even this plan would give half the members of the country to the least capable class of voters; and it would have the additional disadvantage of establishing a poor-class member and rich-class member side by side in the same constituency, which would evidently be likely to excite keen jealousy and perpetual local bitterness.

We believe, indeed, that it was an afterthought in the advocates of " minority representation," to propose it as a means of giving some, but not too much, representation to the poor. Its name shows that it was originally devised as a means of giving a representation to minorities *as such*. The extreme case used to be suggested of a party which had a very large minority in every constituency, but which had not a majority in any, and had not therefore any share in the representation. It cannot be denied that such a case might occur: but if the constituencies be, as they should be, of varied kinds, it is very unlikely; and in politics, any contingency that is very unlikely never ought to be thought of; the problems of practical government are quite sufficiently complicated, if those who have the responsibility of solving them deal only with difficulties which are imminent and dangers which are probable. But in the actual working of affairs, and irrespectively of any case so extreme as that which is put forward, the elimination of minorities which takes place at general elections is a process highly beneficial. It is decidedly advantageous that every active or intelligent minority should have adequate spokesmen in the legislature; but it is often not desirable that it should be represented there in exact pro-

* The rule is, that a minority, to be certain of electing its candidate, must be more than that fraction of the constituency, which may be expressed as follows:

$$\frac{\text{The number of votes.}}{\text{The number of members} + \text{the number of votes.}}$$

portion to its national importance. A very considerable number of by no means unimportant persons rather disapproved of
the war with Russia; but their views were very inadequately represented in the votes of Parliament, though a few able men adequately expressed their characteristic sentiments. And this was as
it should be. The judgment of the Parliament ought always to be
coincident with the opinion of the nation; but there is no objection to its being more decided; it is extremely important that it
should not be less decided. Very frequently it is of less importance which of two courses be selected than that the one which
is selected should be consistently adhered to and energetically
carried through. If every minority had exactly as much weight
in Parliament as it has in the nation, there might be a risk of in-
decision. Members of Parliament are apt enough to deviate from
the plain decisive path, from vanity, from a wish to be original,
from a nervous conscientiousness. They are subject to special
temptations, which make their decisions less simple and consistent than the nation's. We need a counteracting influence;
and it will be no subject for regret if that influence be tolerably
strong. It is therefore no disadvantage, but the contrary, that
a diffused minority in the country is in general rather inadequately represented. A strong conviction in the ruling power
will give it strength of volition. The House of Commons should
think as the nation thinks; but it should think so rather more
strongly, and with somewhat less of wavering.

It was necessary to discuss this aspect of the minority principle, though it may seem a deviation from the investigation into
the best mode of giving a due but not an undue influence to the
working classes. The advocates of that principle generally consider its giving a proper, and not more than a proper, degree of
power to the poor as a subordinate and incidental advantage in
a scheme which for other reasons ought to be adopted; it was
therefore desirable to prove that no such other reasons exist, as
well as that it would very imperfectly, if at all, tend to place
the working classes in the position we desire.

Some persons have imagined that the enfranchisement of all
the lower orders may be obtained without its attendant consequence, the disfranchisement of other classes, by means of
the system of "double representation," which gives to the primary electors only the power of nominating certain choosers, or
secondary electors, who are to select the ultimate representative.
This proposal was made by Hume many years ago; it formed
part of more than one of the earlier French constitutions; and it
is now being tried, as we have observed, in Prussia. We have
an example of its effects likewise in a part of the constitution of
the United States. Although, therefore, we may not have quite

so full a trial of the proposed machinery as we could wish, we have some experience of it. The most obvious objection to it is, that it gives to the working classes the theoretical supremacy as much as a scheme of single representation. Whether the working classes choose the member of Parliament, or whether they choose an intermediate body who are to choose the member, their power of selection will be equally uncontrolled, the overwhelming advantage derived from their numbers will be the same. It is alleged that the working classes will be more fit to choose persons who would exercise an intermediate suffrage; that they could choose persons in their own neighbourhood well known to them, and for whom they had a respect; and that the ultimate representative nominated by these local worthies would be a better person than the working classes would have nominated themselves at first. And in quiet times, and before a good machinery of electioneering influence had been organised, we are inclined to believe that such would be the effect. The working classes might, in the absence of excitement and artificial stimulus, choose persons whom they knew to be better judges than themselves; and, in accordance with the theory of the scheme, would give to them a *bonâ-fide* power of independent judgment. But in times of excitement this would not be the case. The primary electors can if they will require from the secondary a promise that they will choose such and such members; they can exact a distinct pledge on the subject, and give their votes only to those who will take that pledge. This is actually the case in the election of the President in the United States. As a check on the anticipated inconveniences of universal suffrage, the framers of the federal constitution provided that the President should be chosen by an electoral college elected by universal suffrage, and not by the nation at large directly. In practice, however, the electoral college is a " sham." Its members are only chosen because they will vote that Mr. Buchanan be President, or that Colonel Fremont be President; no one cares to know any thing else about them. There is no debate in the college, no exercise of discretionary judgment: they travel to Washington, and give their vote in a "sealed envelope," and they have no other duty to perform. According to these votes the President is elected. Such, indeed, appears the natural result wherever the lower orders take a strong interest in the selection of the ultimate members for the constituency. They have the power of absolutely determining the choice of those members; and when they care to exercise it, they will exercise it. In Prussia, as it would appear from the newspaper narrative of the recent elections, a real choice has been exercised by the Wahlmänner—the secondary electors. But a few years of experience among a phlegmatic people are not a sufficient trial; there are as yet no parliamentary agents at Berlin. In this country, as in America, an effectual stimulus would soon be applied to the primary electors. If twenty intermediate stages were introduced, the result would be identical : a pledge would be exacted at every stage; the primary body would alone exercise a real choice, and the member would be the direct though disguised nominee of the lower orders. This scheme would every where, in critical times, and in *electioneering* countries at all times, give to the democracy an uncontrolled power.

An expedient has, it is true, been proposed for preventing this. It has been suggested that the secondary electors,—the electoral college in the American phrase, — should have other duties to perform besides that of electing the representative. Suppose, for example, that the electors at large chose a municipal town-council, and that the latter elected the representative of the town in the legislature ; it is thought that persons with good judgment would be chosen to ensure the due performance of the municipal duties, and that a good member of Parliament would be selected by the *bonâ-fide* choice of those persons with good judgment. The scheme would be far too alien to English habits and traditions to be seriously proposed for adoption by this country even if its abstract theory were sound; but there is an obvious objection of principle to it. The local duties of a municipal council are too different from that of selecting a parliamentary representative to be properly combined with them. We should probably have a town-council of political partisans, as was the case before the Municipal Reform Act; and the uninteresting local duties would be sacrificed to the more interesting questions of the empire. In the real operation of the scheme very much would depend on the *time* at which the town-council was elected. If it were elected simultaneously with the general election of members of Parliament, nobody would think of any thing but the latter. The town-councillors would be chosen to vote for the borough member, and with no regard to any other consideration. We should have a fictitious electoral college, with the added inconvenience that it would be expected to perform duties for which it was not selected, and to which it would be entirely ill-suited. On the other hand, if the town-council were elected when the parliamentary election was not thought of, we might, in times of fluctuating opinion, have a marked opposition between the opinion of the town-council and the opinion of the constituency. In an excitable country,—and every country which takes a regular interest in politics becomes excitable,—no such opposition would be endured. It would be monstrous that the member for London at a critical epoch, say when a question of war or peace was pressing for decision, should be nominated by a town-council

elected some time before, when no such question was even thought
of. There used in the ante-Reform-Bill times to be occasional
riots when the close corporations, with whom the exclusive suffrage in many boroughs then rested, made a choice not approved
of by the population of the town. If this was the case when the
borough-councillors were only exercising an immemorial right,
it will be much more likely to be so when they are but recently
nominated agents, deriving their whole authority from the dissen-
tients, and making an unpopular choice in the express name of
an angry multitude. We may therefore dismiss the proposed
expedient of double representation with the remark, that if the
intermediate body be elected with little reference to its electoral
functions, it will be little fitted for such functions; and if it is
elected mainly with reference to them, it will have no independent
power of choice, but be bound over to elect the exact person whom
its constituents have decided to favour.

A much more plausible proposal is suggested by the recommendation which we made some pages back,—that the principle
which assigns the franchise to those who can show a property
qualification should not be confined to real estate, but be extended to every kind of property that yielded an income and was
owned *bonâ fide*. A considerable number of the working classes
possess savings; not large, it is true, when contrasted with mid-
dle-class opulence, but still most important to, and most valued
by, those who have hoarded them during a lifetime. The total
accumulation is likewise very large when set down in the aggregate. It has been suggested that a suffrage conferred on the
owners of moneyed property would of itself enfranchise the most
thrifty and careful of the working classes; and that, as these
would probably be the best judging of their class, it would be
needless to inquire as to the mode in which any others could
obtain the franchise. There may be a question whether we do
wish simply to find representatives in the best of the working
classes. We are not now seeking legislators who will exercise a
correct judgment, but rather spokesmen who will express popular sentiments. We need not, however, dwell on this, as there
is a more conclusive objection to the plan proposed. Un-
fortunately, the savings of the working classes are not in-
vested in a form which would be suitable for political purposes.
The most pressing need of the poor is a provision for failing
health and for old age. They most properly endeavour to satisfy this by subscribing to "benefit societies" or other similar
clubs, which, in consideration of a certain periodical payment,
guarantee support during sickness, or a sum of money in case of
decease. Now this life-and-health insurance wants all the criteria of a good property qualification. There is no test of its

bona fides. Simulated qualifications might be manufactured by any skilful attorney. The periodical payment might be easily repaid on pretence of sickness; and it would be perfectly impossible for any revising barrister to detect the fraud. There would be no security that the periodical premium even belonged to the poor man; it might be lent him, and with little risk, by his richer neighbour. Electioneering has conquered many difficulties. It would be easy to have an understanding that the secretary to the society, the clerk of the electioneering attorney, should see that the premium was soon repaid, in name to the poor subscriber, and in fact to the vote-making capitalist. The finances of some of these societies have never been in the best order; and there would be very great difficulty in tracking even a gross electioneering fraud. Perhaps no practical man will question but that the manipulation of a borough attorney would soon change the character of a " benefit society;" it would cease to be, as now, the repository of the real savings of the best working men; it would become a cheap and sure machinery for creating votes in the name of the most corruptible. So large a portion of the savings of thrifty operatives are most properly laid by in these insurance associations, that it is scarcely likely that a moneyed property qualification would give a vote to a considerable proportion even of the very best of them. A few would be admitted by giving the franchise to those who left a certain sum in a savings-bank for a certain time; but, to prevent fraud, that time must be considerable, and careful returns, prepared for Lord John Russell's Reform Bill, are said to show that the number enfranchised would be even fewer than might have been expected. At any rate, it would not be safe to rely on such a franchise for creating a parliamentary organ for the lower classes. Those enfranchised by it would be scattered through a hundred constituencies. There would be no certainty that even one member in the House would speak their sentiments. Moreover, we have doubts whether a constituency composed only of operatives who had a considerable sum in the savings-bank after providing, as in all likelihood they would have done, for the wants of their families in case of their death and sickness, would not rather have the feelings of petty capitalists than of skilled labourers. Those who have just risen above a class can scarcely be relied on for giving expression to its characteristic opinions. However, as it would be scarcely possible to create such a constituency, there is no reason for prolonging an anticipatory discussion on its tendencies. On the whole, therefore, we must, though rather against our wishes, discard the idea of creating a working-class franchise by an extension of the suffrage qualification to all kinds of property. A careful examination appears to show that

c

we could not obtain in that way a characteristic expression for the wants of the masses.

These are the principal schemes which have been proposed for adding to the legislature some proper spokesmen of the wants of the lower classes by giving to those classes *some* influence in every constituency. Our survey of them has confirmed the anticipation with which we set out. The dilemma remains. Either the influence is great enough to determine the choice of the member, or it is not: if it is not, no spokesmen for the working classes will be elected; if it is, no one not thoroughly imbued with the views and sentiments of the lower orders would be chosen,—we should have a democracy.

As this, the first of the only two possible expedients, has failed us, we resort with anxiety to the second. Since it does not seem possible to procure spokesmen for the working classes by a uniform franchise in all constituencies, is it possible to do so by a varying franchise, which shall give votes according to one criterion in one town, and to another criterion in another town? It evidently *is* possible. Whether there are any countervailing objections is a question for discussion, but of the possibility there cannot be a doubt. If all the adult males in Stafford have votes, then the member for Stafford will be elected by universal suffrage; he will be the organ of the lower orders of that place. Supposing that place to be subject in this respect to no important local anomaly, the lower orders there will be like the corresponding classes elsewhere. By taking a fair number of such towns, we may secure ourselves from the mischievous results of local irregularities; we can secure a fair number of spokesmen for the lower orders.

The scheme is not only possible, but has been tried, and in this country. Before the Reform Bill of 1832 there was a great disparity in the suffrage qualification of different constituencies. "A variety of rights of suffrage," said Sir James Mackintosh, in 1818,* "is the principle of the English representation;" and he went on to enumerate the various modes in which it might be obtained,—by freehold property, by burgage tenure, by payment of scot and lot, &c. The peculiar circumstances of 1832 made it necessary, or seemingly necessary, to abolish these contrasted qualifications. Great abuses prevailed in them, and it would have been difficult to adjust remedies for the removal of those abuses. The great requirement of the moment was a simple bill. During a semi-revolution there was no time for nice reasonings. Something universally intelligible was to be found. The enthusiasm of the country must be concentrated "on the

---

* *Edinburgh Review*, No. LXI., article "Universal Suffrage;" an admirable essay, singularly worth reading at present.

whole bill and nothing but the bill." We must not judge the tumult of that time by the quietude of our own.

At a calmer moment the more philosophic of liberal statesmen were, however, aware of the advantages of the machinery which they were afterwards compelled to destroy. The essay of Sir James Mackintosh, to which we have referred, appeared in the *Edinburgh Review,* and was considered at the time as an authoritative exposition of liberal doctrine : and almost the whole of it is devoted to a proof that this system of varying qualification is preferable, not only to universal suffrage, but to *any* uniform " right of franchise." On the point we are particularly considering, he says : " For resistance to oppression, it is peculiarly necessary that the lower, and in some places the lowest, classes should possess the right of suffrage. Their rights would otherwise be less protected than those of any other class : for some individuals of every other class would generally find admittance into the legislature; or, at least, there is no other class which is not connected with some of its members. Some sameness of interest, and some fellow-feeling, would therefore protect every other class, even if not directly represented. But in the uneducated classes, none can either sit in a representative assembly, or be connected on an equal footing with its members. The right of suffrage, therefore, is the only means by which they can make their voice heard in its deliberations. They also often send to a representative assembly members whose character is an important element in its composition,—men of popular talents, principles, and feelings; quick in suspecting oppression, bold in resisting it; not thinking favourably of the powerful; listening, almost with credulity, to the complaints of the humble and the feeble; and impelled by ambition, where they are not prompted by generosity, to be the champions of the defenceless. It is nothing to say that such men require to be checked and restrained by others of a different character; this may be truly said of every other class. It is to no purpose to observe, that an assembly exclusively composed of them would be ill fitted for the duties of legislation; for the same observation would be perfectly applicable to any other of those bodies which make useful parts of a mixed and various assembly." Sir James had evidently the words of the member for Westminster sounding in his ears. His words are not an expression of merely speculative approbation, they are a copy from the life.

An authority still more remarkable remains. Lord John Russell, in 1821, expressed a very decided opinion on the advantages of having a different scale of property qualification in different places, and rather boldly grappled with an obvious objection to it. We quote the passage : " All parts of the country, and all

classes of the people, ought to have a share in elections.   If this
is not the case, the excluded part or class of the nation will become of no importance in the eyes of the rest : its favour will
never be courted in the country, and its interests will never be
vigilantly guarded in the legislature.   Consequently, in proportion to the general freedom of the community will be the discontent excited in the deprived class by the sentence of nullity and
inactivity pronounced upon them.   Every system of uniform
suffrage except universal contains this dark blot.   And universal
suffrage, in pretending to avoid it, gives the whole power to the
highest and the lowest, to money and to multitude; and thus
disfranchises the middle class,—the most disinterested, the most
independent, and the most unprejudiced of all.   It is not necessary, however, although every class ought to have an influence in
elections, that every member of every class should have a vote.
A butcher at Hackney, who gives his vote perhaps once in twelve
years at an election for the county of Middlesex, has scarcely
any advantage over another butcher at the same place who has
no vote at all.   And even if he had, the interest of the state is
in these matters the chief thing to be consulted ; and that is
as well served by the suffrage of some of each class, as by that of
all of each class."   The necessary effect of the Act of 1832 has
been to make us forget the value of what the authors of it considered a most beneficial part of our representative system.   That
such great statesmen should have pronounced such panegyrics
on the diversity of qualifications in different constituencies, when
it was a living reality before their eyes, shows at least that it is
practicable and possible.

The plan is, indeed, liable to several objections : it is not to
be expected that in a complicated subject any scheme which is absolutely free even from serious inconveniences could be suggested.
By far the most popular objection is that which Lord John Russell noticed in the passage we have just cited.   There is a sense
of unfairness in the project.   Why should an artisan in Liverpool have a vote, and an artisan in Macclesfield no vote?   Why
should the richer classes in one constituency be disfranchised
by the wholesale admission of their poorer neighbours, and the
richer classes in another constituency not be so disfranchised?
The answer is suggested by a portion of our preceding remarks.
No one has a right, as we have seen, to any portion of political
power which he cannot exercise without preventing some others
from exercising better that or some greater power.   If all the
operatives in the great towns were enfranchised, they would prevent the higher classes from exercising any power : and this is
the reply to the unenfranchised artisan in Macclesfield.   If there
were no representatives of the working classes in Parliament, its

measures might be less beneficial, and its debates would be imperfect; the higher classes in some great towns must have less power than in some other great towns, because a uniform suffrage impedes the beneficial working of Parliament, and prevents the ruling legislature from exercising its nearly omnipotent power well and justly. To have a good Parliament, we must disfranchise some good constituents. Perhaps, indeed, the whole difficulty is overrated. We see every day that, so far as the middle classes are concerned, it is of no perceptible consequence to the individual whether he has a vote or not : it is of great consequence to him that the supreme legislature should accord with the views of his class and himself; but whether he has voted for any particular member of that legislature is a trifle. We never dream in society of asking whether the person we are talking to has a vote or not. Both live, and live equally, in the atmosphere of politics. Similarly, it is of great importance to the lower classes that their feelings should be sufficiently expressed in Parliament; but which of them votes for the person who should express them is of no consequence at all. The non-voter ought to take as much interest in politics as the voter. When *all* of a class cannot exercise power without impeding a more qualified class, we may select from considerations of convenience which members of the less qualified class are to have power. There is no injustice in allowing expediency to adjust the claims of persons similarly entitled.

It may also be objected that this plan of representing the lower classes does not give them the general instruction which the exercise of the suffrage is supposed to bestow. An unenfranchised artisan in Macclesfield is not educated by giving the suffrage to an artisan in Manchester. But it is a mistake to suppose that there is much, if any, instruction in the personal exercise of the franchise. Popular elections have no doubt a didactic influence on the community at large; they diffuse an interest in great affairs through the country; but the elevating effect of giving a vote is always infinitesimally small. Among the lower classes it is a question whether the risk of moral deterioration does not quite equally balance the hope of moral elevation. Popular institutions educate by the intellectual atmosphere which they constantly create, and not by the occasional decisions which they require. And were it otherwise, intellectual instruction is but a secondary benefit of popular government; and we must not throw away, in the hope of increasing it, the primary advantage of being well governed. We believe too that, in fact, mere existence under a good government is more instructive than the power of now and then contributing to a bad government.

We are more afraid of the objection that this inequality of suffrage in otherwise similar constituencies is an anomaly which may grow up imperceptibly, as it did before the Reform Bill, but cannot now be created *de novo.* We admit the difficulty : we are well aware that this inequality, like every other expedient in politics to which the objections are apparent and the advantages latent, is far easier to preserve than to originate. But when great interests are at stake, we should only give up that which is impossible; what is merely difficult should be done. Moreover, a little examination will, we think, show that the obstacles are far slighter than they might seem at first sight.

In this point of view it is worth remarking, that the inequality of suffrage qualification to a certain extent still exists. The operation of the Reform Act has been to hide and diminish, but not to annihilate, the inequalities which existed before. The constituencies in which these inequalities existed were naturally opposed to their abolition, and a compromise was effected. All persons duly qualified to vote on the 7th of June 1832 were to retain their right for life, subject to certain conditions of residence and registration. In all boroughs, likewise, in which freedom of the borough, whether acquired by birth or servitude prescriptively, gave a vote, that franchise was to a certain extent retained. The freemen of such boroughs have votes now just as before, and freedom can be acquired in the same way : no change on this point was effected in 1832, except that a borough franchise so obtained is forfeited by non-residence in the borough. The number of these anomalous votes is still very considerable. Mr. Newmarch has shown that in 1853 it amounted to 60,565, which is more than one-seventh of 400,000, the number (or nearly so) of borough electors at that time. We have therefore a very considerable amount of inequality in our present system; we should scarcely propose to increase it, but to distribute it more usefully.

The freemen of Coventry, Derby, Leicester, are not a class of whom we wish to undertake the defence ; and in many towns the existence of those old rights is a recognised nuisance. We are not prepared to approve *all* anomalies in our representation. Our principles are especially opposed to the enfranchisement of favoured individuals in minor towns—few enough to be bought, corruptible enough to wish to be bought,—who are not in general the majority of the constituency, but who exercise important influence because they can throw in a purchasable balance of votes on critical occasions ; who are in no respect fair representatives of the working classes, who do not return to the house a single fit person willing to be spokesman for them. We argue only that the effect of the Act of 1832 has been to diminish the inequality of suffrage qualification before existing; and by no means to establish, even if a single act of parliament could have so done, the erroneous principle that there is to be no inequality.

But the most effectual way of showing that it is possible to create *de novo* a beneficial variety of property qualifications, is to point out how it can be done. If it be admitted that we should found working-class constituencies, it is clear that we should found them where the working classes live. This is of course in the great seats of industry, where work is plentiful and constant. Those who reside in such towns are likewise the most political part of the class : the agricultural labourers, scattered in rural parishes, with low wages and little knowledge, have no views and no sentiments which admit of parliamentary expression ; they have no political thoughts. If we wish to give due expression, and not more than due expression, to the ideas of the democracy, we must select some few of the very largest towns, where its characteristic elements are most congregated. It would have been more fortunate if these towns had acquired such a franchise prescriptively; but it would have been all but miraculous if such had been the case. Many of our greatest towns are situated in what, in more purely agricultural times, were very uninfluential districts; we must not expect an hereditary franchise for newly-created interests. As it is necessary to have a rule of selection, the best which can be suggested is the rule of population; we would propose, therefore, that in the very largest towns in England* there should be what Mr. Bright advocates for all towns, a rate-paying franchise. If this were extended to all towns having more than 75,000 inhabitants, it would include London, Liverpool, Manchester, the Tower Hamlets, Marylebone, Finsbury, Bristol, Birmingham, Lambeth, Westminster, Leeds, Sheffield, Wolverhampton, Southwark, Greenwich, Bradford, Newcastle-on-Tyne,

---

* It may, indeed, be objected that these large constitnencies are just the ones in which a rate-paying franchise would have the most conclusively democratic effect; and that if we concede it as to these, it is not worth while to resist it with respect to others in which we might hope, by the influence of wealth and social standing, to counteract more or less its democratic tendency. But facts show that in an immense number of constituencies these influences could not control that tendency effectually. If an act giving votes to all rate-payers be ever passed, it will probably be accompanied by a readjustment of the electoral districts on a democratic principle, which would augment the influence of mere numbers. But we need not consider this, since the introduction of the rate-paying franchise into our present constituencies would introduce a new element, much too large to be easily managed by indirect influences. It is of course not known exactly how large that new element would be; but very careful tables have been compiled of the number of inhabited houses in our present boroughs; and as the number of women rated in respect of them is no doubt small, all but a minute fraction of such houses would give a qualification to a male voter. Now it appears that in all except ten borough constituencies the number of inhabited houses was in 1852, and doubtless is still, more than double that of the present electors; and consequently the *new* element which would be introduced would greatly pre-

and Salford. If there were a *bonâ-fide* representation of the working classes in these towns, they could not complain of a class disfranchisement; there would be adequate spokesmen for them. A member speaking the voice of places where such numbers of operatives are congregated, could speak the sentiments of that class with authority. No one could be unaware that the constituency in these large towns was ultra-democratic. The representation of the lower orders would be conspicuous as well as effectual.

Nor would the number of representatives so given to the lower classes be sufficient to deteriorate the general character of the legislature. It would not amount to forty for England and Wales, or to fifty for the United Kingdom; a considerable number, no doubt, but not sufficient to destroy the representative character of a house of 658 members. The House of Commons would still represent the educated classes as a whole; its opinion would still be their opinion; the performance of its ruling function would be unimpaired; and that of its expressive function would be improved.

We have dwelt so long on this part of our subject, that we shall not be able to devote as much space as we could wish to the explanation of the mode in which we think the remaining defects of our representative system should be remedied. We can only state briefly a few of the most important considerations.

The first of those defects, which we specified at the outset, is

ponderate over, and in fact disfranchise, the old. It is evident that it would be very difficult to manage so many new voters by any indirect influences. We copy the table for two counties, Cornwall and Lancashire.

CORNWALL.

	Electors.	Inhabited Houses.
Bodmin	390	1,103
Helston	309	1,459
Launceston	438	1,051
Liskeard	372	965
Penryn and Falmouth	856	2,073
St. Ives	536	2,003
Truro	646	2,194

LANCASHIRE.

	Electors.	Inhabited Houses.
Ashton-under-Lyne	1,085	5,346
Blackburn	1,518	7,919
Bolton	1,933	10,394
Bury	1,218	5,825
Clitheroe	457	2,192
Oldham	2,098	13,658
Lancaster	1,328	2,891
Rochdale	1,255	5,829
Warrington	720	4,380
Wigan	797	5,686

—*Edwards's Statistical Tables*, p. 6.

the existence of small boroughs, which are either in the hands of individual proprietors or have become in the process of time nests of corruption. We need not specify examples; the fact is sufficiently familiar. Indeed, all small boroughs in the course of years must rapidly tend towards one or other of these fates. A great deal of wealth in this country seeks to invest itself politically. A small borough of this sort necessarily contains a considerable number of corruptible individuals; year by year skilful parliamentary agents ascertain who these individuals are, and buy them. The continual temptation is too much for shop-keeping humanity; with every election the number of purchasable votes tends to increase: one would not have yielded, only he wanted a new shop-front; another, who is proof against plate-glass, desires money to put out his son in the world. Gradually an atmosphere of corruption closes over the borough, and men of the world cease to expect purity from it. The only way in which this sort of retail purchase can be escaped is by a wholesale purchase. A rich proprietor may buy a large majority of the vote-conferring properties in the borough, and so become despotic in the town. Each presentation (to borrow a phrase from the church) is not in that case sold on the day of election, because the advowson has been bought before by some one who has a use for it.

We may escape, then, the necessity of ascertaining the electoral corruption of particular boroughs, and lay it down as a general condition of permanent purity that a constituency should contain a fixed number—five hundred suppose—electors. It is quite true that this remedy is not certainly effectual: there are many boroughs, where the enfranchised constituency exceed this number, in which the elections are not at all what we should wish. But the tendency of such a measure is plain. It prevents the wholesale purchase by the neighbouring proprietors, because it makes the property too large for all ordinary wealth to buy. It *tends* to prevent the retail purchase by increasing the supply of votes,—which always lessens their market value, and in very many cases reduces it below the price which will tempt ordinary voters to corruption. The expedient is not a perfectly effectual one, but at the least it is a considerable palliative.

What, then, is to be done with boroughs below the prescribed limits? There are in England and Wales about sixty-seven members, elected by forty-two of such boroughs. What course would it be wisest to take with respect to such seats? The most easy plan in theory is to annihilate them at once, to have a new schedule A of places disfranchised. But it is easier to write such a recommendation in an essay than to carry the enactment in practice. These seats have the protective instincts of property.

Money has been spent on many of them for a course of years: in all of them the present electors would vote nearly as a man against the abolition of "themselves." The strenuous resistance of the members for such seats must be expected to any bill which should propose to abolish them *in toto*. And such resistance would be the more effectual, because in all likelihood it would be indirect. The interested members, unless a sinister policy were unusually wanting in its characteristic acuteness, would not risk a division on the unpleasant question of abolishing or not abolishing their own seats. They would throw the probably decisive weight of their votes into the scale most inconvenient to the government proposing that abolition; would combine with every strong opposition to it; in the present state of parties would soon reduce it to a minority. A proposal to disfranchise many boroughs would soon issue in the resignation of the proposing government.

We must therefore assume that for the present, to some considerable extent, the influence of such boroughs must continue to exist. In 1832 there was a popular feeling which carried every thing before it. Now all we can hope to carry is a compromise. As a compromise, the best expedient which we can suggest is to combine such boroughs. The English respect for vested interests would preclude the popularity of a sweeping act; but the English liking for a moderate expedient would be a strong support to any measure that could be so called. The effect of such a combination would probably be in great part to set the joint constituency free from the yoke of great proprietors. If Lord A is supreme in borough *a*, and Mr. B in town *b*, *a* and *b* combined will probably be controlled by neither. The local feeling of *b* will resist Lord A; that of *a* would be rigid to the enticements of Mr. B. If one of the boroughs should be "independent," that is to say, purchased voter by voter at each election, its inhabitants would probably rather be purchased by any one than by the proprietor of the antagonistic borough. We are aware that these are not very attractive considerations; but what are we to do? *ils ont des canons.* We must make the best terms we can with constituencies which we cannot hope entirely to destroy.

We shall be asked why we group these existing boroughs with one another, instead of combining them with new towns not now possessed of the borough franchise, which are therefore at present comparatively uncorrupt. We admit that, in some individual cases, there may be conclusive reasons for taking the latter course; but we think that there are political arguments which should disincline us from adopting it in general.

We saw reason to believe that the principal defects of our

House of Commons, as a *ruling* assembly, were an excessive bias to the landed interest, and an insufficient sympathy with the growing interests of the country. On this account it is desirable not to take from the county constituencies all the liberalising element which they at present possess; on the contrary, it would be desirable, if possible, to increase it. We should, however, weaken that liberal element very materially if, in our extreme desire to remedy borough corruption, we extracted from the constituency of the counties the inhabitants of all their larger towns. The effect of Mr. Locke King's proposal to reduce the county franchise from 50*l.* to 10*l.*, if it should be adopted, as it probably will be, will be to augment the county influence of the towns which have no borough member.* We must not counteract this tendency. As we think it desirable to diminish the *sectarian* character of our county members, we must not adopt the most effectual of all schemes for preserving it unimpaired—we must not absorb into the boroughs all other influences save those of the country gentlemen.

Our second reason for rather preferring to combine the very small boroughs with one another than to unite each of them with some town at present unenfranchised is, that we wish to diminish the number of seats for such constituencies. If we annexed new elements to each of them, there would be a plausible argument for not diminishing their number. But, as has been explained, we wish to provide a more ample representation for the growing districts of the country; and there is a very general and well-grounded opinion that the House of Commons is already quite sufficiently numerous. In order, therefore, to increase the representation of the progressive parts of England in the proportion which seems desirable, we must take from the decaying or stationary towns of the less active parts of the country the right of sending members which they have now. On a great scale, the same plan was adopted in 1832: it was then necessary to remedy a great evil; and therefore it was necessary that the number of seats disfranchised should be great, and the number of newly-enfranchised towns considerable also. As we have shown, no such enormous evil remains at present to be remedied. The judgment of Parliament coincides fairly, if not precisely, with the opinion of the nation. All we have to correct is, a slight bias in one direction, and a perceptible but not extreme

---

* The general effect of Mr. Locke King's proposal is a *quæstio vexata.* One point may be, however, laid down with confidence : its effect will probably be more favourable to the petty proprietor than to the large ones. The estates of the larger are not usually cut up into farms yielding less than 10*l.* rent. The small occupier generally rents of the small proprietor. Possibly the effect of this circumstance, likewise, may be to mitigate the class peculiarities of our county members. The quarter-sessions influence varies with the acreage.

deficiency of sympathy in another. The changes we have to make, therefore, may be slight in comparison with those of 1832; still, so important is it that Parliament should really coincide in opinion with the nation, that we should take account of the beginnings of a discrepancy; while the topic of reform in our electoral system is definitely before the public, we should take the opportunity of correcting the undue inclination of the legislature towards the less active, and its contrast of feeling (which though slight is real) to the more active part of the community.

We are the more certain that it is advisable to make some such change as this, because, as we have before observed, we believe this uneasy consciousness of the less perfect representation of the progressive elements in the nation, as compared with the unprogressive, to be the secret source of almost all the slight popular enthusiasm which now exists in favour of reform. The external form of what is proposed is, indeed, different; the principal, as well as the most popular, suggestion is one for the representation of the working classes. We have no doubt that those who are at the head of that movement, as well as those who join in it, quite believe that such is their true object. But it is at least an odd undertaking to be headed by master manufacturers. Whatever view we may take of the effects of universal or of rate-paying franchise on other parts of the nation, there can be little question that its influence would be detrimental to the power of opulent capitalists. We must alter the world before there ceases to be some opposition of feeling (there is often a momentary opposition of *interest*) between the mill-owner and his work-people. In the days of the short-time agitation both parties understood this perfectly. Even now a Parliament of capitalists would probably propose to repeal the ten-hours bill; a Parliament of working men would very likely desire to extend its principle. To say the least, it is strange that the characteristic men of one class should be so ready to throw all power into the hands of the other.

A letter from Mr. Bright himself to a Manchester association puts the matter in a different light. "On a great occasion," he tells us, "like the one now before the country, there will be differences of opinion. Some think one extent of franchise better than another. Some are for a 6*l.* rental; some are for a 5*l.* rental; you are for the extension of the right of voting to every man. Now I prefer to establish the parliamentary suffrage on the basis which has been tried for some centuries in our parishes, and which has been adopted at a recent period in our poor-law unions and in our municipal governments; with some needless restriction, with regard to the municipal franchise, which I would not introduce into our parliamentary franchise. The more public opinion is freely and honestly expressed, the more distinctly will a government, engaged in preparing a Reform Bill, be able to discover which is the point likely to be most satisfactory to the public. I consider these differences of opinion on the subject as of trifling importance when compared with the question of the distribution of seats and members. *This is the vital point in the coming bill;* and unless it be well watched, you may get any amount of suffrage, and yet find, after all, that you have lost the substance, and are playing merely with the shadow of popular representation."

This at least is an intelligible doctrine. A redistribution of seats in proportion to population would indisputably be most advantageous to Mr. Bright and his associates. Some of their school have made a calculation that sixty-three boroughs, returning eighty-five members, have not, taken together, as many electors as Manchester, which returns but two. And, independently of extreme cases, it is quite indisputable that the large towns and crowded populations of Lancashire and the West Riding would, in any grouping based on electoral numbers, assume a proportionate magnitude that would be quite different from that which they have at present. If such a readjustment could be carried, *and the present franchise retained,* the followers of Mr. Bright would be one of the most numerous divisions of the House of Commons. It is true that the advantage of their success must be shared with the class most antagonistic to them in feeling. The county representation would have to be extended if electoral numbers, or any mere numbers, were to be taken as the guide to a new adjustment. But Mr. Bright probably does not fear a conflict with Mr. Newdegate. We can well understand that he should esteem the lowering of the franchise, which would impair his power, less important than a reapportionment of members, which must increase it.

We can spare but a few words to show the unsoundness of the principle on which the proposed readjustment is to be based; and we would hope that only a few words are needed. Mr. Bright considers it an obvious absurdity that a constituency of 1000 electors should return a member, and that another constituency with 5000 should return but one member also. Such a variety is nevertheless *primâ facie* beneficial: it would be a probable sign of the complete imperfection of an electoral organisation if every constituency in it were equally numerous. All such systems must tend to give undue preponderance to some classes, and to deny, not only substantial influence, but even bare expression, to the views of other classes. If the nation be homogeneous, equal patches of population will tend to return similar members. The more numerous the constituency, the more likely is this to be the result. Thousand A *may* differ from Thousand B; but Million A will assuredly be identical with Million B. The doctrine of chances forbids us to expect contrasted representatives from constituencies with a family likeness. If, indeed, the nation should not be homogeneous, but should contain two very numerous classes of unlike tendencies, whose harmony is preserved by the continual arbitration of less numerous classes intermediate between them, the result of an equal division of electoral districts would be different, and it would be worse. Each of the intermediate classes would be merged in one of the larger. We may, however, look at the living operation, and not at the bare theory. We have mentioned the contrast between Mr. Bright and Mr. Newdegate. What is it that prevents the continual disturbance of parliamentary peace between two classes of men so dissimilar as the members for counties—especially purely agricultural counties—and members for manufacturing cities? Obviously the existence of the intermediate elements, of members sent up by agricultural towns, which contain industrial elements, and by smaller manufacturing towns, which have no notion of being offered in sacrifice to the populace of great cities. An electoral system composed of " population sections" would not give us a representative assembly adapted to the performance of either of its two functions. A House of Commons so elected would not represent the public opinion of the country, and therefore could not rule it as it should be ruled. The impartial and arbitrating element would be deficient. And, as has been explained, this complete deficiency in the qualities necessary to a ruling legislature would not be compensated by any excellence in the qualities necessary to secure a good expression of the grievances and opinions of all classes. Old English good sense selected a town to send representatives separately from a county in which it was situated because it saw there the conspicuous focus of separate feelings, separate interests, possibly separate complaints. Our new reformers would undo this wise arrangement. They would (at least, such is the logical tendency of their argument) destroy those bounds and limits to constituencies which secure a *character* to the constituency; they would represent the shipping interest by throwing Hull into the county of York and Grimsby into the county of Lincoln: distinct definition is all that is necessary to disprove such ideas.

Paradoxical as it may sound, the evident untenableness of Mr. Bright's views gives them a claim on our attention. It is an indication of social unsoundness that men of ability and energy sincerely advocate very absurd theories, and are able to collect considerable audiences to applaud those theories. We may speak of our national contentment; but the answer comes, What, then,

do these people complain of? We must not rest satisfied with
a mere refutation of the doctrines which are avowed, or an exposition of the mischievous consequences of the plans proposed.
There are certain theories of political philosophy which supply
ready arguments against almost every state of society which has
been able to maintain a long existence. These heresies float
among the most ordinary ideas of mankind, and are ready without the least research to the hand of whoever may believe that
he wants them. Latent discontent with the existing form of
government catches hastily at whatever justifies it; it seeks in
these old forms of false doctrine a logical basis for itself. One of
these heresies is the purely democratic theory of government;
it has very rarely indeed been adopted as a guide to action, but
its existence is nearly as old as political speculation. In every
age and country a class which has not so much power as it thinks
it ought to have snatches at the notion that all classes ought to
have equal power. Such an "uneasy class" believes that it ought
to have as much power as the class which is in possession; and
not liking to put forward even to itself a selfish claim of individual merit, it tries to found its pretensions on the "equal rights
of all mankind." Mr. Burke described the first East-Indian
nabobs as "Jacobins almost to a man," because they did not
find their social position "proportionate to their new wealth."
We cannot fail to observe that the new business-wealth of the
present day (of which Mr. Bright is the orator and mouthpiece)
has a tendency to democracy for the same reason. Such a symptom in the body-politic is an indication of danger. So energetic
a class as the creators of Manchester need to be conciliated; their
active intelligence has rights which assuredly it will make heard.
The great political want of our day is a *capitalist conserva-
tism.* If we could enlist the intelligent creators of wealth in
the ranks of those who would give their due influence to intelligence and property, we should have almost secured the stability
of our constitution; we should have pacified its most dangerous
assailants; we should count them among our most active allies.
If the transfer of a moderate number of seats in Parliament
from boroughs, which scarcely profess to exercise an independent
choice of representatives, to large and growing towns would only
in a subordinate degree conduce to this effect, such a transfer
should be made. There would still be enough of smaller constituencies for all purposes that are useful.

We have, therefore, completed our task. We have shown
the defects which our present system of representation seems to
contain; and we have endeavoured to indicate the mode in which
those defects might, we think, be remedied. The subject is one
of great complexity and extent, and very difficult to discuss

within the limits of an article. To be considered profitably, it must be considered as a whole; and it will be evident from our own pages how much space any attempt to discuss the entire topic necessarily requires. Whatever errors of detail may be found in our opinions, we cannot doubt that our general purpose has been correct. A real statesman at the present day must endeavour to enlarge the influence of the growing parts of the nation, as compared with the stationary; to augment the influence of the capitalist classes, but to withstand the pernicious theories which some of them for the moment advocate; to organise an expression for the desires of the lower orders, but to withstand even the commencement of a democratic revolution.

NOTE.

18th February 1859.

THERE are some points suggested by the previous discussion which I was unable, from want of space, to treat as I should have wished; and some too which have been brought out more clearly by the events of the last few weeks. I gladly, therefore, make use of the opportunity afforded me by the republication of the foregoing essay to make some additional remarks.

A striking and most healthy symptom in the public mind in reference to Reform just now is its *freshness.* In former times the Tory party never thought about the matter. One of their traditional tenets, as a party, was an opposition to Reform; and all who desired a further change than that of 1832 were in their eyes Radicals and Democrats. The subject was not one for argument. The Liberals, on the other hand, had a vague kind of abstract idea that the franchise must be extended some time or other. They would have been shocked to hear themselves called Democrats; but when they talked about Reform, their language, as far as it had a meaning at all, had a democratic meaning. It was imagined that as soon as the "masses" had acquired a certain minimum of education, they would have a claim of right to be enfranchised; and it was overlooked that in practice this would be equivalent to the disfranchisement of all other classes, and would give the lower orders the uncontrolled guidance of the community. At present the state of public opinion is infinitely more hopeful. The Tories have been stimulated to the consideration of the subject. As a government of their own is to propose a Reform Bill, it is impossible any longer to regard the topic as beyond the range of permitted speculation. The Liberals likewise have been rather rudely awakened to the unpleasant consequences of their former ideas. Mr. Bright, more than any one else, should have the credit of arousing the present liberal reaction against democracy. He has propounded in a definite plan what was before an intangible idea. The subject has come within the range of practical English thought almost for the first time; and, as usual, the tone of habitual discussion on it has deepened and improved. A feeling of sympathy for intelligent working people is perhaps stronger than ever, and there is every wish that they should, if possible, have some power in the community; but there is a distinct and settled determination that they shall not have all the power.

I have dwelt so fully on this part of the subject in the preceding essay, that it is not necessary for me now to resume the general discussion of it. The public mind is in a much more likely mood to entertain what appear to me to be just ideas than it ever was before, or than I could have hoped it would be now. There are one or two incidental remarks, however, which it is necessary to make on the subject.

The most telling objection to the expedient suggested in the foregoing essay for representing the working classes—viz. that of lowering the qualification so as to include them in the great seats of industry, but not elsewhere—is, that it sacrifices the political power of the higher classes in those important places. The higher classes in Manchester cannot be expected to *like* that they should be disfranchised by the wholesale enfranchisement of the working men in Manchester. That it should ever be pleasant, it would be impossible to hope; but there are some considerations which tend, I think, to make it less unpleasant than might be imagined at first sight.

In the first place, a great deal of the anticipated calamity has happened, and is being endured. The creators of the wealth of Manchester,—and when I speak of Manchester, I only do so because it stands out in the public mind as a type and symbol of cities of the class,—are not the ten-pound householders who return its members. These are the small shopkeepers and petty dealers, who swarm and congregate about every great commercial place; but who bear to the merchants and manufacturers of those places much the same relation that the sutlers of a camp bear to its disciplined army. In London, where the geographical division of industrial pursuits is unusually evident, there are whole constituencies composed nearly exclusively of these rather mean attendants on commercial civilisation. The Tower Hamlets contain very little else; and any one can see by walking

D

through them how little their population has of the cultivated energy and enlarged acuteness commonly to be found in a great merchant. In other towns—Liverpool is a striking contrast in this respect to London—this attendant community of inferior dealers resides in the closest proximity to the most important mercantile offices—in the focus of business transactions. The effect of the Act of 1832 has been to throw the representation of the large trading towns into the hands of these inferior traders, whose vicinity to the greater ones is inevitable, and whose numbers are overwhelming. A portion of the higher class of traders sympathise in the views of the lower; this portion assume to be the leaders of the place, and give to persons at a distance an idea of its tendencies quite different from what would be desired by the higher citizens in general. There has always been an anti-Manchester party at Manchester. The school which Mr. Bright represents has not the undisputed lead among the manufacturing and mercantile men of the north which they are commonly thought to have. The most cultivated people there are perhaps generally opposed to it. The highest and best class of the traders in great commercial towns are already disfranchised ; and it would, in reality, be better for them that it should be thoroughly understood to be so. At present the world imagines that their present representatives express their feelings, and state their opinions. If the representation of such places were avowedly and constitutionally in the hands of the working classes, it would be understood that the higher traders had no voice. Those of them—and they are a very large number—who have none now would be great gainers, because they would no longer have the vexation of being thought to sympathise with persons to whom they are emphatically opposed. The reason is different with respect to the prevailing party in those boroughs; but the conclusion is the same. So far are Mr. Bright's followers from protesting against the wholesale admission of the class of voters just below them, that they are clamorous in favour of that admission. If the adoption of a rate-paying franchise is supported by any part of the country, it is by the constituencies of the very largest towns. There is no hardship in giving to them the boon which they demand for every one.

If, however, it should be found that the higher classes of the largest towns exceedingly disliked the evident disfranchisement which would be the certain consequence of extending the borough franchise in such towns to the lower orders, it would not be by any means impossible to find practicable plans of preserving to them an effectual franchise. The first of these plans is the creation of what may be called *suburban* constituencies. The greater part of our merchants and traders, even the higher part of our shopkeepers, have long since deserted the straitened dwellings over the shop and the counting-house which contented their fathers. They have residences in country districts near their places of business; all round our largest cities there is a network of them. Many constituencies could be found in the environs of our great cities where the rich, comfortable, and intellectual business-classes reside in very great numbers, and where they would be far more likely to predominate, and to have an effectual voice in the selection of members of Parliament, than under the present suffrage system they are, or can be, in the great seats of industry themselves. Such classes would benefit exceedingly by conceding to the working classes the undisputed command of the representation of the great town itself, if they could thereby obtain a real representation for themselves at their own homes. That which they have now—so numerous are the meaner householders—is rather a vexing mockery than a desirable reality; what they would obtain would be a substantial and effectual influence on the legislature. If it were necessary, it would be easy to provide that the representation should be really in the hands of the higher class by fixing the property qualification for a vote at a higher point than usual (at 20*l.* suppose); but I rather apprehend that this expedient, though quite defensible, and by no means intrinsically undesirable, would not be absolutely necessary, as the number of the higher classes residing in well-selected suburban constituencies would give them, under a ten-pound franchise, an effectual superiority.

A second plan, which is not inconsistent with the first, but rather supplementary to it, is a development of the suggestion that personal property should be made the basis and criterion of a qualification as well as real property. The first step to carry this into practice raises the question, For what constituency is this qualification to give a vote? Railway debentures and the public funds have no locality; if they are to give a vote, they may do so for one place as well as for another. I would propose to give the voter himself a choice on this point. If he had the power of registering himself on the ground of a monied-property qualification within a certain circle of constituencies,—say to any one situated at not more than fifty miles from his usual place of abode,—he could transfer his vote to that one where it was most wanted, and would be most effectual. The higher classes in the largest constituencies—practically disfranchised as they almost are now, and as they would be quite if the suggestions I have ventured to make were adopted—might find a satisfactory refuge in the smaller constituencies of the neighbourhood, whose numbers they would augment, and whose composition they would materially improve. In general, too, the crea-

tion of a *transferable* constituency, by conferring the suffrage
on the possessors of non-local wealth *as such*, would be a mate-
rial strengthening of the educated classes as opposed to the non-
educated, because it would give the former an opportunity of
concentrating their power where it would tell most, while the
power of the lower classes would be dispersed, and inseparably
attached to certain places.

Both of these are expedients for giving to the disfranchised
upper classes of the most numerous constituencies power *elsewhere* than in these constituencies; two other expedients may be
mentioned, by which they might still retain considerable influence *in* them.

The first of these is a modification of the " minority principle." It has been shown in the preceding essay, by arguments
which are to my own mind conclusive, that this ingenious expedient would not of itself solve the problem of giving to the working classes a certain number of spokesmen in Parliament without conferring on them the supreme authority in the state. The
working classes are the enormous majority in the country; if
the franchise is universally lowered so as to include them in every
constituency, they will be masters of the country. By means of
the minority principle a certain power may be preserved to some
fraction more or less of the constituency, according to circumstances; but the great preponderance will be with the majority
still. In the case usually supposed of a constituency with three
members, in which each constituent has nevertheless but two
votes, a minority at all greater than two-fifths of the constituency could return one member, if they pleased it, with complete
certainty; but the corresponding majority of a trifle less than
three-fifths would return two members with equal certainty.
The influence of the majority would still be double the influence
of the minority. So far from this principle giving to the working
classes a few members and no more, it gives the greater number
to them, and only a few in comparison to the rich. But though
this expedient does not of itself give the solution of the problem
of which we are in search, it gives us the means of alleviating
the inconvenience attaching to what we have found to be one
solution of that problem. We may by means of the minority
principle give a voice to the rich in the exceptional constituencies in which it has been proposed to lower the franchise so as
to include the working men. In these constituencies we only
wish to give the rich some power; it is the principle of the proposal to give the greater power to their inferiors.

One of the modes in which the minority principle might be
made use of for this purpose has an appearance of equality which
would be, I should imagine, attractive to consistent Democrats.

It is proposed that, no matter what the number of members for the constituency may be, no elector shall have more than one vote. As has been previously pointed out, this is by far the most efficacious form of the minority principle, because the minority to which it gives a member is smaller than it is under any other modification of that principle. If there were only two members for a constituency, a minority at all exceeding one-third might be certain of returning a single member. I cannot, indeed, imagine that in this form the principle could ever be adopted, or even seriously advocated. No one would say that one-third *plus* one of the nation was entitled to as much voice in its deliberations and decisions as two-thirds *minus* one of it. A small minority, as such, and no matter how composed, could never claim to have as much power as a large majority, the members of which might, for aught which appears, be equally intelligent. Nor, even if we supposed the minority to be the rich and educated, and the majority the poor and ignorant, would the result be satisfactory. The error would then be in the other direction: the ignorant majority would in that case have as much power as the instructed minority, which is exactly what we desire that they should not have. Like all other modifications of the minority principle, this one fails as an anti-democratic expedient applicable to the whole country. It would be most dangerous to lower very greatly the franchise throughout the country, in reliance on its efficacy in precluding a despotism of the uneducated. But if the franchise be only extended to the working classes in certain exceptional constituencies, the adoption of the rule that no elector should have more than a single vote might in them be very beneficial. Suppose that three members were assigned to such constituencies, and that no elector possessed more than a single vote, a moderate fraction (one-fourth of the constituency *plus* one) could always be sure of returning a member, and the remaining part of the constituency (three-fourths *minus* one) would return the other two. If the higher classes of a great town were really united, and used their legitimate influence with zeal, they could always command somewhat more than a quarter of the constituency: they would be secure of returning a representative to the legislature as well as their inferiors.

The same end would be reached by the adoption of what is called the "cumulative vote" in these exceptional constituencies. By this is simply meant that the elector should be permitted to give all his votes to a single member if he pleases: thus, if the members to be elected for the constituency be three, and each elector have three votes, he would be enabled to give all his votes to any one candidate, instead of being compelled, as at present, either to distribute them among three candidates, or abstain from using some of them. By means of this expedient also, a minority at all greater than one quarter could with certainty return a member; and the effect in that respect would be of course the same as if that result had been attained by the other expedient. I cannot but think, however, that the latter mode is very preferable in other respects. Mr. J. S. Mill says very justly that the principle of giving the elector fewer votes than there are members to be elected must always be unpopular, "because it cuts down the privileges of the voter;" while, on the other hand, the adoption of the cumulative vote increases them, and has in consequence a tendency to be popular. Mr. Mill justly observes also that the expedient of the "cumulative vote" has another great advantage; it enables voters to indicate not only their preference for a candidate, but the degree of their preference. Instead of voting mechanically for all the candidates put forward by their party, it enables them to select the one whom they really themselves most approve, and to support him only. This would tend to secure to eminent and trusted statesmen a secure position in their respective constituencies, which is one of the most important among the minor excellencies of a representative system.

By one or other of these two schemes, it would be possible to give a real representation to the working classes in the large towns in which they live, and to preserve a portion of influence and a share in the local representation to the higher classes of the town. Both schemes are, however, liable to the very considerable objection that they permit, or rather provide for, the election in the same place of a member for the poor and a member for the rich, which is very likely to cause local ill-feeling, and may sometimes irritate the poor into momentary turbulence. On this ground, it seems to me preferable that the higher classes in the large towns should be content with such indirect compensation for their local disfranchisement as would be afforded by the two plans which were noticed first. But popular impression has an incalculable influence in such questions; and if the higher classes in these first-class constituencies would feel it a stigma or an injustice to have no share in their local representation, such a share must be reserved to them, although we are thereby compelled to allow of the election of two contrasted kinds of members for the same town.

It may likewise be objected to the creation of such exceptional constituencies as I have proposed, that their exceptional character could not be permanent. If you once lower the qualification in one constituency, it may be said there will be no rest from agitation until it has been lowered to the same extreme point in all constituencies. But this appears to me to assume

that the democratic tendencies of the country are far more powerful than they really are. The extension of the suffrage, especially a very large extension of it, is not very popular with the
existing constituencies. If we give to such privileged bodies a
good argumentative defence, the oligarchical tendencies of human
nature will go far to ensure their maintaining their privileges.
Nothing tends to the longevity of a public benefit so much as
its being also a particular private advantage to some one who
will look after it. Such a defence the existing constituencies
will really have if we assign to the working classes some real representation in Parliament; but while the most numerous class
have no means at all of making their voice heard, there will
always be an uneasy feeling that they are unduly depressed and
unfeelingly disregarded. So far, then, from the creation of exceptional constituencies tending to weaken the arguments in favour of the general structure of the present constituencies, it is
the only way of removing the most telling argumentative objection to our existing arrangements.

An exceptional character in particular constituencies is, it
should be observed, an essential element in every system of *class*
representation. If you lay down the principle that there shall
be persons in Parliament qualified and authorised to speak the
sentiments of special classes, you must take care that in certain
electoral bodies those classes shall predominate, that the member for such bodies shall be their member. You can only secure
speciality in the member by a speciality in the constituency.
This is the very ground on which borough populations were originally selected for a separate representation. It was believed
that places differing so much from the rural districts in which
they were situated would have distinct interests to advocate,
distinct opinions to maintain, possibly distinct grievances to
state. In a word, it was believed that they would send a special
representative, with something to say different from that which
an ordinary county representative would ever say. By selecting
for particular representation towns occupied in all the important
kinds of trade, we have secured an expression to the opinions
and sentiments of all kinds of capitalists. By giving special representatives to the universities, we have provided, perhaps
not adequately, but still to some extent, for the characteristic
expression of the peculiar views of the cultured classes. I
believe that the principle of special representation should be extended to the lower classes also, who, from an improvement in
education, have now in the larger towns opinions to state, and
perhaps, in their own estimation, grievances to make known. If
a special representation is given to such persons, it can only be
in the same way that special representatives are given to other

classes, by creating constituencies with a corresponding speciality.

It is to be observed, that the necessity for creating such
exceptional constituencies would not be obviated by the recommendation which Mr. Mill has made of giving one vote to every
man, whatever be his education, and additional votes in a rapidly-
ascending scale to persons of greater education. The object of
this recommendation is to keep the principal authority in the
state in the hands of educated men. The scale of votes is avowedly arranged for that purpose. By the adoption of this scheme,
you would give to the working classes no characteristic expression in the legislature; you would give them an influence
in every constituency in appearance considerable, but which
would be of no practical avail to them as a class, because on all
characteristic points their voice would be neutralised, and when-
ever there were class candidates theirs would be rejected, by the
more numerous votes given for that very purpose to the more
educated classes.

I must have wearied every reader with this part of the subject; and my only excuse is the strong conviction which I feel
of its importance, and my wish not to omit to make any observation which may serve to throw it into what seems to me the
true light.

The only other point on which I wish to say any thing more
has reference to the rival schedules of Mr. Bright and of the
Times. I own I cannot imagine that any such extensive scheme
of disfranchisement as either of these two plans contemplate is
at all within the sphere of practicability. There is no such
pressure from without as could alone compel the passing of a
measure so destructive. Nor upon principle does it seem to me
that the adoption of such a scheme would be advisable. The
principle, both of Mr. Bright's schedules and those of the *Times,*
is the disfranchisement of the smaller constituencies, whether
corrupt or uncorrupt, whether independent or dependent; and
the transfer of their members to very large towns or to counties. As far as the nomination boroughs go, I have no wish to
say a word in their defence. In former times there may have
been a certain advantage in the existence of such seats. Young
men of promise were then occasionally brought into Parliament
by the patrons of such constituencies, and great statesmen
sometimes found a refuge in them during moments of unpopu-
larity. But these advantages belong to past times. Before the
Reform Act of 1832 the borough proprietors had boroughs to
spare; such was the plenty of such seats, that there were some
left for the public, after providing for the relations and personal
friends of the proprietor. But the fact is otherwise at present.

There are not now enough of such boroughs to provide for the
personal connections of those who own them; and the public
derive almost no advantage from their continuance.

As I have explained, all very small boroughs tend to become
either dependent or corrupt, and therefore all very small ones
should be abolished. But this is no ground for abolishing a great
number of constituencies which, though not very large, are still
large enough to be fairly independent and fairly uncorrupt.
There can be no ground for disfranchising every place which
has not 10,000 inhabitants. If we look to abstract principle as
our guide, no measure would be more undesirable. We have
seen it to be desirable not only that there should be special
representatives for every class in Parliament, but likewise that
the predominant tone and temper of Parliament should be des-
potically controlled by no class or sect of persons, that it should
coincide with the feeling of the nation itself. The accordance of
the opinion of Parliament with that of the country is the principal condition for the performance by Parliament of its great
function of ruling the country. This can only be secured by
the continuance in Parliament of many members representing no
special interest, bound down to state the ideas of no particular
class, themselves not markedly exhibiting the characteristics of
any particular *status*, but able to form a judgment of what is
good for the country as freely and impartially as other educated men. It is impossible to expect that such persons will
be commonly sent to Parliament by the counties and the large
towns. A good deal has already been said of the *sectarian*
character of the county members. I fear it must be allowed
that the better class of members for large towns are at least as
sectarian; they are capitalists, men of business, representing
the views and opinions of the ten-pound householders. I am
not speaking of such members as stray in occasionally for such
constituencies as the Tower Hamlets. A low class of demagogue
will now and then be returned by every very large constituency;
but the characteristic tendency of the large towns is to return
men of business of mature age, and of a certain very recognis-
able, if not very describable, tendency of sentiment and opinion,
—a kind of member as marked, as peculiar, and as distinct
from all others as any county member can be. I cannot but
think that we shall impair the proper working of our parliamentary constitution if we greatly augment the number of class representatives, whether for the large towns or the counties. Whatever other defects may be alleged to exist in the smaller boroughs,
the objection that they return exclusively the representatives of
a class cannot be made to them. Every species of member sits
for some of them. A list of persons more unlike one another

E

could hardly be found than the list of the representatives for our smaller boroughs. When we consider how exceedingly important it is that the judgment of Parliament should be alloyed by no class prejudice or class interest, that its decisions should be in accordance with the real and deliberate decision of the nation, we shall, I hope, pause before we abolish constituencies so likely to contribute to effect this result. It is not possible for human skill to apportion to each special interest the exact number of representatives which it ought to have, and to compose a Parliament exclusively of such special representatives. It would require more skill than any statesman can claim to establish a coincidence of opinion between Parliament and the country solely by the definite allotment of particular members to particular classes. There is no criterion to tell us with accuracy how much each class contributes to the formation of public opinion. The sole expedient for securing the result which we wish to obtain, is that by which it has actually been obtained. We have a Parliament, subject to two slight objections, fairly coincident in judgment with the reflecting part of the community. This inestimable coincidence of judgment is largely due to the immemorial existence of very many impartial constituencies. We have class advocates in Parliament, it is true; but many unbiased judges, many national representatives, are to be found there likewise. Perhaps no course could be more dangerous for the country than to diminish the number of the latter, and so lose, possibly at a very critical moment, the incalculable benefit of their impartial intelligence.